"Stay right next to me and remember I have a gun pointed at you," the man said. "I don't think you want someone innocent to be hurt because you did something foolish."

As they walked side by side with Bree slightly in front, she felt the barrel of the weapon pressed into her. She calculated her chances of getting away from the gunman now that they were outside in the parking lot and fewer people were around. But she couldn't come up with anything that didn't end with him shooting her in the back.

When Bree was a few feet from the driver's side of the gunman's car, she reached to open the door.

"Drop the gun or I'll shoot you." David's voice came from behind them.

The man shoved the gun barrel into her back. "Not if you don't want me to kill her." He swung around with Bree plastered against him with one arm across her chest to hold her in place. "I'm leaving with her."

David lifted his arm and pointed his revolver at the gunman's head. "You won't survive."

"Neither will she," he retorted.

Books by Margaret Daley

MARGARET DALEY

feels she has been blessed. She has been married more than thirty years to her husband, Mike, whom she met in college. He is a terrific support and her best friend. They have one son, Shaun. Margaret has been writing for many years and loves to tell a story. When she was a little girl, she would play with her dolls and make up stories about their lives. Now she writes these stories down. She especially enjoys weaving stories about families and how faith in God can sustain a person when things get tough. When she isn't writing, she is fortunate to be a teacher for students with special needs. Margaret has taught for more than twenty years and loves working with her students. She has also been a Special Olympics coach and has participated in many sports with her students.

THE YULETIDE RESCUE

MARGARET DALEY

HARLEQUIN® LOVE INSPIRED® SUSPENSE

Recycling programs
for this product may
not exist in your area.

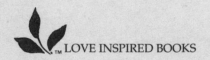 LOVE INSPIRED BOOKS

ISBN-13: 978-0-373-67648-4

The Yuletide Rescue

www.Harlequin.com

Printed in U.S.A.

Be strong and of a good courage; be not afraid,
neither be thou dismayed: for the Lord thy God
is with thee whithersoever thou goest.
—*Joshua* 1:9

To my friend Helen,
who showed me the beauty of Alaska

ONE

In the bush plane high above the Alaskan landscape northwest of Anchorage, Dr. Aubrey Mathison swept her gaze over the barren snow-covered terrain below, the endless white broken by evergreens and leafless trees. Even through the headset she wore, she heard the loud droning noise of the engine saturate the cockpit.

She glanced toward the east as the sky grew light. Streaks of purple, rose and orange fanned outward as the sun rose at ten-thirty in the morning. The sight awed her. God's beauty stretched for miles before her.

"I think these trips to the villages are one of my favorite parts of my job," Bree said to the pilot sitting next to her in the single-engine aircraft. She'd spent a month in Daring, Alaska, on the Bering Sea. Now it was time to go home to Anchorage for some rest and relaxation.

Jeremiah Elliot slid a glance toward her. "It's why I love to fly. Nothing beats the view."

Jeremiah was more than just her neighbor; he was like an uncle to her. He'd been her father's best friend for years and had watched out for her and her mom after Dad died eight years ago. She'd been thankful for Jeremiah since she'd spent a lot of time away from Alaska not long after her dad died while she'd been attending medical school.

"But I'm glad to be returning home." Bree glanced toward Jeremiah.

He winced, deep grooves carving lines into his aged, weatherworn face.

Alert, Bree sat up. "Something wrong?"

"Just indigestion. I've flown feeling worse than this. No doubt I shouldn't have eaten that third helping of pancakes before takeoff."

"Three helpings! You need to watch your weight. Your metabolism is slowing down as you get older."

"Quit being a doctor," Jeremiah grumbled and rubbed his arm. "Sixty isn't that old."

"Maybe we should land before Anchorage."

"No way. I'm tough, and a little heartburn isn't going to get me down."

She released a long breath. "Uncle Jeremiah—"

"Girl, don't you call me that. It won't work. You're as bad as your mom when she wanted her way." He looked at her, his mouth set in a frown.

Bree sent Jeremiah a grin. "At least I come by it honestly." The thought of her recently deceased mother not being with her this Christmas dimmed her smile. She turned to stare out the windshield as Jeremiah flew low over the treetops.

"I have to drop off some Christmas presents at a friend's cabin, and that's the only stop we'll make before reaching Anchorage."

"Is your friend's place here?" She pointed to the ground.

"No, just wanted you to see that moose down below. Beautiful animal."

As Bree admired the moose, Jeremiah pulled the plane up higher. He would often go up and down to show her something interesting. "You know I need to learn to fly. Will you teach me?"

"Sure, when summer comes. Don't have to deal with snow and ice then."

"Not to mention subzero temps."

A half hour later, Jeremiah landed the ski plane on a section of flat snowy ground near a frozen stream not far from a cabin. "I'll be back in a few minutes." He shifted in the seat and grabbed a bag.

Bree glimpsed the brightly wrapped packages before he closed the sack and climbed from the plane. She watched as Jeremiah trudged uphill through the deep snow toward the cabin nestled among the black spruce trees. He disappeared around the side of the cabin and came back into view ten minutes later.

Jeremiah knew people all over Alaska and often helped them out. Although this wasn't a place she'd seen before, she was acquainted with a lot of his friends. Some of them lived in the outlying villages he took her to for her month's rotation as the doctor. She scanned the area. Beautiful but isolated. She hadn't seen much on the approach but wilderness.

Jeremiah opened the door and pulled himself into the plane, his face red from the cold, his breathing hard. Settling behind the controls, he donned his headset and let out a whoosh of breath. Walking in deep snow could exhaust a person quickly, and Jeremiah looked as if he had gained an extra twenty pounds in the past six months.

"Okay?" she asked as the sound of the engine filled the quiet.

He scowled. "I'm fine." Then, without another word, he took off, using the flat land next to the stream as his runway.

"What plans do you have for the holidays?" Bree asked after ten minutes of silence had passed between them. The silence was so unlike Jeremiah, who usually talked through the whole flight.

When he didn't answer, she looked at him. Sweat beaded Jeremiah's face, and his complexion was now a pasty white. Bree's concern returned tenfold. "Jeremiah, you should see your doc—"

He jerked, but his hands still gripped the controls. The plane dropped altitude quickly.

Was he having a heart attack? Her medical training kicked in immediately, but along with it came panic. She knew nothing about flying a plane. "Jeremiah, what can I do?" she asked as she removed one of her thick gloves and felt for his pulse at the side of his neck. It raced beneath her fingertips.

Pain scored his face. He fumbled with a switch, then said, "Mayday. Mayday."

As the ground rushed up at them, Bree was unable to do anything but pray. She swiveled her attention between an approaching open space that looked to be a small frozen lake and Jeremiah. From what she could tell, he must be having a heart attack but was hanging on as long as he could to land the plane. If not...

Bree shook that thought from her mind. *Lord, help. Please.*

Clutching the seat, Bree prepared the best she could for a rough emergency landing. The skis touched down on the frozen terrain, but the plane bounced up, then down again. Finally, the single-engine aircraft slipped and slid over the frozen lake as it plunged toward the huge trees lining part of the shore. Jeremiah wrestled with the steering, trying to control the plane.

Then, pain contorting his face, he stopped struggling and slumped forward.

Bree's grip on the seat tightened as the plane plowed into the trees and rocks along the lake's edge. All she saw was green hurtling toward her, then everything went black...

Seconds, possibly minutes later, pain and a biting cold sliced through the darkness shrouding Bree's mind. She wanted to burrow back down into unconsciousness, but the sounds of the wind howled through the cockpit. Pellets of ice and snow found her uncovered face, further prodding her to wake up. She inched one eyelid up and glimpsed the jagged edges of the windshield. A branch, several inches thick, lanced through the glass like a spear.

Then realization pierced through the haze of soreness. *Jeremiah.* She tried to sit up, but a limb off the bigger branch, filled with clusters of short needles, pinned her against her seat.

She brought up one arm next to the door and tugged on the annoying foliage, hoping to break it off. Finally she managed to bend it until it snapped; then she tossed it into the back of the aircraft.

Bree undid her seat belt and turned to find Jeremiah. Her medical bag was in her larger piece of luggage in the belly of the plane, which was now lying on the frozen lake, the skis having been ripped off on impact. But she knew Jeremiah had a first aid kit in the cockpit. First, though, she wanted to check on him. Squatting on her cushion, she leaned over the intruding branch, parting the limbs. Jeremiah wasn't moving. Her heartbeat pounded in her chest and head. She pulled off her glove and felt for a pulse through the greenery.

Nothing.

Fighting panic, she gathered her strength, gripped the branch and shoved it out the hole it had created in the windshield. The effort caused her head to swim. Plopping back against her seat, she closed her eyes for a few seconds. Something wet trickled down her face, and she wiped at it with her gloveless hand.

Blood covered two of her fingers. Then she glanced at her chest and noticed the red that spattered her tan coat. She probed her forehead and found a cut about an inch long. After wiping her hand against the front of her parka, she slowly sat up and searched for her cell phone in her front pocket. When she turned it on, the screen gave off some much-needed light. She needed to get to her bag and retrieve her flashlight. No bars, but then she hadn't expected any service in the middle of nowhere.

She drew in a deep breath of frigid air to calm her racing pulse. She knew fear and panic inspired frantic actions that zapped a person's strength fast. Conserving her energy for the necessary tasks was important.

Using the light from her cell phone, she leaned toward Jeremiah, praying he was alive and she just hadn't been able to find his pulse a couple of minutes ago.

"Please, God, let him be alive. Please," she whispered.

When she had determined he was gone, she sank back in her seat. Before she could even react, she was swamped by pain that no doubt had been masked by the rush of adrenaline from the emergency landing. The throbbing in her head increased, making it difficult to think. She was alone, somewhere between Daring and Anchorage. Why hadn't she paid more attention to where Jeremiah was flying? She usually was alert while traveling to a new village, but on the ride home, weariness would sometimes overtake her and occasionally she'd fall asleep.

Light from the snow surrounding them shadowed Jeremiah's body as it lay slumped over the steering wheel. To conserve the battery, Bree switched off her phone. She could still make out the trees in front of them and a sloop to the left of the grove of evergreens. From somewhere in her mind came a bizarre thought: if only she had an app for heat.

Staying in the plane wasn't an option with the wind ripping through it and the possibility of the ice cracking beneath it and the aircraft sinking into the frigid water. She had to find shelter. Shelter near the plane, because of the aircraft's emergency transmitter. To do that, she needed the emergency supplies that were stored in the rear of the cockpit.

After rummaging through her duffel bag as well as Jeremiah's—luckily they weren't in the inaccessible cargo bay—she gathered what she could use to keep warm as well as her flashlight. She lit the cabin and zeroed in on the survival kit. She would stuff each bag with what she needed to make it through the long night ahead. She knew the growing darkness and stormy weather would make it unsafe for rescuers to search for her.

Jeremiah had always stocked a couple of extra provisions not required in the new regulations. She spied the shotgun with a box of ammunition and immediately felt better. Her father and Jeremiah had often taken her hiking in the backcountry and had taught her how to shoot. She knew the dangers a bear could pose.

Before leaving the aircraft, she grabbed the first aid box and tended to the cut on her forehead, scrubbing at the blood that had frozen on her skin. She placed a large bandage over the wound and pulled her hat back down over her head to keep any body heat from escaping.

She peered at Jeremiah in the pilot seat and felt emotion finally break through. Tears stung her eyes. She couldn't believe he was gone. He always transported her to and from the villages and had been there to help her through her father's and mother's deaths. Never again. A tightness in her chest spread upward to jam her throat. Tears rolled down her cheek and froze, pulling her up short, reminding her of the harsh environment she faced until she was rescued. She touched Jeremiah's shoulder, saying a brief prayer and a heartfelt goodbye. The safest thing was to stay near the plane because of the emergency transmitter's signal.

After tossing the duffel bags to the ground, followed by the survival kit, she put on the snowshoes, not sure how deep the snow was by the lake, and exited the plane. In the light of day—she prayed it would be early tomorrow—the bright red wings would help searchers in the sky find her. At least that was what she prayed for, but she did have a signaling device in the emergency kit if needed.

"Bree, stop thinking ahead. See to now," she muttered and trudged a few yards from the wreckage. She could see the plane sat mostly on land; only the tail rested on the frozen lake. She forced herself to plan ahead. Doing so always gave her a sense of security.

Make it back to Anchorage—then figure out your future.

Behind some evergreens, the shore of the lake sloped upward with a denser stand of trees at the top of the rise a couple of feet back. She peeked through the foliage and made a decision. To the left in the middle of the incline was where she would dig her snow cave. Using a collapsible shovel from Jeremiah's survival provisions, she began digging, keeping her mind focused on the task at hand. Ninety minutes later, with breaks to rest, eat a protein bar and drink some water, she finished the crude shelter she'd learned to make in her survival training class.

She stacked the duffel bags to block the entrance after she crawled inside, taking her shovel with her. After she lay down on the sleeping bag, which was spread out over a tarp, she turned on her flashlight and examined her snow cave. She'd curved the walls and poked some holes in them to allow fresh air to enter.

The small confines triggered a childhood memory. She'd been exploring a tight cave when her light had gone out, leaving her in the darkness with little wiggle room. At the memory, she began panting, her fear returning. Usually closed spaces didn't bother her, but suddenly she struggled with the image of the cave in her mind. She had to do something to keep herself calm. She began singing her favorite Christmas songs.

By the time she finished "I'll Be Home for Christmas," she couldn't shake the question: What if she wasn't? The cracking of ice mingled with the howling of wolves in the distance.

She pulled up her legs and clasped them. *I'm not alone. You're with me, Lord.*

A crashing noise overrode all others. Bree braced herself as though the ground would move beneath her.

His alarm sounded on his watch, and David Stone punched it off and rose from the black leather couch where he'd been trying to sleep. He looked out the window of the hangar that overlooked the small airport near downtown Anchorage, where the Northern Frontier Search and Rescue Organization was based. The wind and snow that had plagued the area since yesterday had finally lessened. He turned away to check on the weather between here and McGrath. The area two hundred miles away where a Mayday call had been sent from a pilot, Jeremiah Elliot.

After hearing from the weather service that there was a break in the storm, David moved quickly toward his Cessna in the hangar. He'd already stocked it during the night. Two people's lives were at stake, the pilot and his passenger, Dr. Aubrey Mathison. He knew of her because of her work in the remote villages. He hoped Jeremiah hadn't crashed and had managed to land somewhere safely. However, all attempts to radio the plane had failed. He hated knowing people were out there in trouble and not being able to rescue them immediately because of severe weather.

David finally took off from the airport and flew northwest. Teams on the ground were headed now in the direction of the emergency signal transmitting from Jeremiah's plane. By the time he reached the area where the plane had gone down, the sun would have risen and visibility should be good, unless the stalled storm behind the one yesterday began moving again. The window to rescue the doctor and Jeremiah could be a narrow one—only hours.

As the sun painted the sky with brilliant colors, he started his grid search, flying low enough to scan the terrain for a down plane or any signs of people.

David gripped the controls as the wind and air currents created a rough ride. He swung his attention between the gauges and the landscape below. Following a snow-covered stream snaking its way through the rugged land, he came to an open area, most likely a frozen lake. Across it he spied a plane partially submerged. The ice had cracked and the tail had sunk into the water.

He flew toward the wreckage to scout the terrain for the best place to land. Through the trees he saw a pack of wolves circling a section of a hill sloping away from the shoreline. Immediately he recognized the dire circumstances the survivors were in—if either of them were still alive.

David flew back around to assess the risk in landing. From the evergreen trees, he could tell the wind blew at least twenty miles an hour. With the threat of crosswinds, he had to choose his approach carefully.

He checked the activity of the wolves. So far they were keeping back from the hole in the hillside where he hoped the survivors had taken refuge, but that could change quickly. David reconnoitered the countryside around the lake for a safe place to land rather than touch down on the snow-covered ice. Generally, the middle of a lake was the strongest, but there could be exceptions, and he wasn't sure the ice would hold.

He found a narrow patch of land maybe a mile away that he could use. Trees surrounded the area, and there were only two directions he could land—northwest to southeast or the reverse. The limbs swayed in the wind, and if the crosswinds were too much, he wouldn't be able to.

He hoped this worked because if it didn't, and he was forced to land in the middle of the lake, he didn't know how he would be able to get to the people who needed to be rescued. The shoreline wasn't thick enough to hold Jeremiah's plane. Would it hold a person?

David lined his Cessna up to go in, panning the sky around him. To the west clouds grew dark, indicating the storm was coming in faster than he hoped. His window of opportunity to rescue Jeremiah and Dr. Mathison was narrowing even more. As he headed down toward the ground, he clutched the controls, fighting the crosswinds threatening to flip him over or drive him into the frozen earth.

About ten yards off the ground, he couldn't hold his course and pulled the nose of his plane up. The bottom of his wheels barely missed scraping the tops of the trees.

One more pass. If that didn't work, he'd have to check on the weather movement and decide whether to land on the precarious lake or return to base and hope the teams on the ground would reach the survivors soon.

Fear held Bree immobile as she listened to the growls outside her snow cave. Her back plastered against the duffel bags in the opening, she gripped the loaded shotgun. She had extra ammunition in her front pocket and a knife in the other one. If the wolves managed to break through her barrier, she would defend herself as best she could.

"Get back," she yelled, swiveling around to point the weapon out a small hole. "If you don't, I'll shoot."

The wolves continued to yap and growl. A brave one came into the hole leading to her opening, blocking most of the light. Aiming down into the snow to avoid killing the animal if possible, she squeezed the trigger and the blast exploded from her gun. The wolf yelped; then silence followed. She peeked through the gap no bigger than a half-dollar and saw the animal backing out.

Shaking, she eased her grip on the shotgun, her hands aching. Her heartbeat thundered a fast staccato rhythm in her ears, almost drowning out another sound—the welcomed sound of a plane flying overhead. She prayed the pilot could make out the wreckage despite the fresh snow that had fallen overnight. What if the aircraft had sunk totally into the water, taking with it Jeremiah's body? She'd wanted to check this morning because all night long she'd heard the creaking of the ice. But then the wolves had arrived.

And the pack was getting braver as the minutes ticked away.

Bree listened for more sounds of the plane overhead. Nothing. And the wolves were still outside her snow cave. The sun no longer shone. Although darkness wouldn't fall for another few hours, the light had dimmed. Was more bad weather moving in? If so, her rescue would be delayed further.

But someone knew where she was—at least she thought so. She clung to that hope even when another wolf returned to the opening, its low growls sending shivers down her spine.

A gunshot cracked the air. She peered through a gap in the bags. The wolf was gone.

The person in the plane? Had he found her after all?

Another blast pierced the cold air, accompanied by a yelp.

Then more silence.

"Help! I'm in here," Bree shouted. She slowly removed the bags from the entrance and crawled from her haven.

When she emerged from the snow cave, the wind whipped against her and her gaze latched on to white bunny boots. Lifting her head, she trekked upward past black extreme-cold pants and parka to a face covered by a balaclava and a pair of dark goggles. The lone man must be six-three or six-four, with a muscular physique. Her attention fixed upon the revolver in his gloved hand.

Friend or foe? Her heart seemed to stop beating for a couple of seconds, then it raced.

TWO

David stared down at Dr. Aubrey Mathison, and she peered up at him with huge brown eyes widened by fear. He'd seen that look many times over his twenty years in the military. Removing his goggles, he smiled. "I'm here to take you and Jeremiah back to Anchorage, Dr. Mathison."

She blinked, transfixed for a long moment.

"The wolves are gone. They won't be back." *I hope.*

She fit her hand in his outstretched one. When he tugged her up, she scanned the area. Through the dense evergreens, her attention fixed on the aircraft, partially submerged in the water, the front end clinging to the shore as though glued to the ground. "Jeremiah's dead," she murmured in a thick voice.

"In the crash?"

"No, I believe he had a heart attack." She

swung her gaze to his; pain reflected in her eyes' expressive depths.

"I'm sorry. Jeremiah was a good man. He'd assist occasionally with air searches when we needed extra help."

"We?"

"The Northern Frontier Search and Rescue. I'm part of that organization." David glanced to the west and frowned. "We'd better get out of here. A storm is moving in. My plane is about a mile from here. I didn't think it was safe to land on the lake."

She stared at Jeremiah's aircraft. "He saved my life. He managed to land even when he was in pain. The ice didn't crack until last night. I heard it from my snow cave."

"Good thing you didn't stay in the plane and you made yourself a shelter."

"God was looking out for me. Let me get my duffel bags."

While she crawled back into her snow cave, David traipsed a few feet closer to the plane at an angle to the left and looked through the stand of trees between him and the lake. All evidence of Aubrey's footprints yesterday along the shore was gone. Inches of new snow blanketed the landscape.

He'd need to let the authorities know about the conditions for when they retrieved Jeremiah's body. Through the broken windshield of the plane, he saw the older man slouched over the steering wheel. He'd seen his share of death while serving in the Middle East, but it was always hard, especially when he knew the person. A memory threatened to worm its way into his thoughts. He slammed it back into the past.

"I wish there was a way to take him back with us."

At the sound of the doctor's voice, he turned. "Me, too, but we need to leave now." He closed the short distance between them and handed her a thermos of water. "Drink this. I don't want you to get dehydrated."

"Thanks. What water I had I finished last night. The wolves came before I built a fire to melt some snow."

After she returned the jug, David took both of her bags. "Let's go."

"I can at least carry one." She tried to take the nearest duffel, but he declined.

He started up the incline, his grip firmly in place on both handles. "I doubt you slept much if any last night. I'm rested, hydrated and well fed."

She slogged behind him. "I had several protein bars with the last of my water. I was conserving the rest in case I wasn't rescued right away, especially when the storm continued through last night. I had to clear my entrance every hour."

"And never warmed up?"

"I spent ten minutes shoveling drifts away from the snow cave, then fifty minutes huddling in the sleeping bag with all the clothes and blankets I could pile on me."

"A long night," David said as he crested the rise circling the lake and started for the thicker wooded area a couple of yards away.

The repetitive sound of a helicopter's rotary blades caused David to stop and turn at the edge of the snow-caked grove of evergreens. No one he'd contacted while organizing the search was in a helicopter. Maybe they were fleeing the winter storm, then had spotted the down plane and were coming to help.

Something instinctively prompted him to step back in the shadows of the trees, pulling the doctor with him. Then he waited for the chopper to come closer. It slowed and hovered over the wrecked aircraft. The chopper was all white with no visible markings on it. He thought instantly of a covert mission. But here? Why Jeremiah's plane?

"Shouldn't we let them know I'm okay?" she asked, taking a step forward.

He urged her back. "No. I'll radio in when we get back to the plane that you're safe. The people searching by air are using planes, but with this storm they should be returning to their base, as we should be."

Suddenly two men, dressed totally in white, lowered themselves to the ground using ropes. Rifles were strapped across their backs and each one also had a sidearm. The hairs on David's nape stood up, and his gut roiled.

Although he and Aubrey were a distance away with a stand of trees between them and the other men, she opened her mouth as if to yell something to the two guys. David dropped one duffel bag, clapped his gloved hand over her lips and hauled her back against his chest, moving deeper into the woods so the slope partially hid them, too. He leaned down and whispered, "Don't say anything. This doesn't look right."

A faint spicy scent wafted to him and for a second riveted his attention. But then he caught sight of one of the men wrenching the pilot's door open and yanking Jeremiah out of the cockpit, then passing him to the other guy on the ground. David stiffened. The way they tossed Jeremiah about wasn't how a rescue team would treat a body.

Snow started falling from the dark clouds overhead, but not quickly enough to erase Aubrey's and his footsteps from the incline behind the trees along the shore. He prayed the men focused on the wreck and nothing else. At least the one in the chopper holding the gun kept his gaze trained on what was going on down at the aircraft.

She wiggled in his embrace, her mumbles muffled by his glove. He dragged her even farther into the trees until he could only see the guy in the helicopter perched in its opening.

With instincts born from many years in a combat zone, David knew they'd left without being seen. Had the people in the chopper heard of the downed plane and decided to plunder it? Whatever their purpose for being here, it wasn't a good one. At any moment they could spot the footprints heading away from the snow cave and come after them, especially if they decided to search the area. He prayed the men would see the urgency in fleeing the storm, which was predicted to be worse than the small one that had come through yesterday.

The farther away from the lake he hauled Aubrey Mathison, the harder she fought him. He was barely able to clutch one of her duffel bags. When they were far enough away from the unknown men, where they couldn't hear Aubrey and him talking, he released her, but he was ready to stop her if she started back the way they'd come.

She yanked away and swung around, fury

darkening her beautiful face. The last time he'd seen her at the rescue of a young child, it had been summer and her blond hair had been pulled back in a ponytail. He'd admired her then, and he did again now with fire shooting from her eyes.

"Did you see how they manhandled Jeremiah like he was a slab of meat?"

"Yes, and that's why we aren't throwing a welcoming party for them." He glanced over his shoulder and lowered his voice, although the wind would carry the sound of their voices away from the men by the lake. "We need to get to the plane and get out of here. Something isn't right. I'll tell the authorities what happened and let them sort it out."

She peered down at the one duffel bag. "You left one back there? It had some of Jeremiah's possessions that I—"

"Yes. I'm sorry about that, but I had more important things on my mind." He hoped the chopper didn't fly over that area and see the snow cave or the duffel bag.

The red in her cheeks from the cold deepened.

"I'll make sure the people who come back later search for it and give it to you. Okay?" He swept his arm wide, indicating the direction she should go.

With a huff, she spun around and charged forward angrily. Whether at him or the two men, David couldn't tell. Amid the snow still coming down, he quickly caught up to her and walked in the same path he'd used to come to the lake. It made his trek a little easier, and he noticed Aubrey did the same thing.

Other than the howl of the wind, silence reigned between them as they plowed through shin-deep snow. The effort slowed Aubrey's pace.

"Is it much farther?" she finally asked, weariness weaving its way through her voice.

"Through those trees about a hundred yards. There's a small clearing where I managed to land my plane."

The sound of the helicopter lifting up above the lake propelled David into action. He grabbed her hand and half ran, half dragged Aubrey to the trees as the chopper appeared in the darkening sky. It headed toward Anchorage, in the opposite direction from them.

David held his breath, waiting to see if the helicopter's flight pattern would continue southeast, away from where his plane was parked north of the lake. When it stayed its course, he hurried Aubrey along as quickly as possible. His revolver and her shotgun were no match for the heavily armed men. What concerned him the most was the increased velocity of the wind, the dropping temperature indicated on his watch and that they had probably half an hour of remaining daylight.

Aubrey stumbled and went down in the snow on the edge of the clearing where his Cessna was. He turned to her and lifted her up, snow all over her parka, face and head covering. Drawing her toward him, David brushed his gloved hand across her cheeks and forehead. The urgency of their situation heightened a connection with her. Any earlier anger was gone, replaced with worry on her face.

She attempted a smile that faded almost instantly. "Sorry. My legs feel like two pieces of lead."

"I know." He wished he could do more to reassure her they would be all right. At the moment he wasn't sure. He held her for a few seconds while she regained her balance. "Okay?"

She nodded, and her gaze bound to his. "You don't need to worry about me. I'll make it to your plane."

David grinned, determined to make it back to Anchorage with her. "Good. Make sure you follow exactly behind me." He emerged first into the clearing and headed for his plane at the other end.

Halfway there, he glanced over his shoulder

to check on Aubrey. Her resolve battled deepening lines of exhaustion. But she kept going, and his admiration of her rose with each step.

The falling snow increased. What light they had was dimming quickly.

"I'm going to hurry ahead and ready the plane for takeoff so when you arrive we can go," David said, then quickened his pace.

David walked around the Cessna and checked what he needed, then climbed into the cockpit as Aubrey reached the plane. She hoisted herself into the passenger seat in front and shivered as she shut the door.

The storm clouds released even more snow as the minutes ticked away and he prepared for takeoff. After starting the engine, David threw her a look. "This may be a bumpy ride and a steep ascent, but we have enough room to make it over the trees."

"I won't be sorry to leave this place." She laid her head against the seat and closed her eyes.

David took off and skated just above the treetops at the end of the clearing. He blew out a long breath, wishing he could relax. It was impossible with the wind battering the plane. His grip tightened on the steering wheel as he flew toward Anchorage, ahead of the storm, he hoped.

Before radioing the airport in Anchorage, he

slid a glance toward Aubrey. Her head slumped to the side; exhaustion must have taken over. *Good.* After what she'd gone through the past twenty-four hours, he didn't want her to see his worry about this leg of their journey.

The line of trees on the shoreline rushed toward Bree as the plane slid across the ice-covered lake. She squeezed her eyes closed and braced for the impact, unable to do anything but pray.

A bump jolted Bree awake, and her eyes flew open. Darkness surrounded her, and for a few seconds, she didn't know where she was. She sat up straight, her muscles locked into place, and blinked at the lit-up controls in front of her. She was safe. It had been a dream. *A flashback,* she corrected.

Then the plane hit another rough patch, bouncing her up and into the door.

"Sorry about that. The storm is on our tail, but we're almost to Anchorage. We'll be fine."

David Stone's deep voice, full of assurance, came to her, calming her racing heartbeat. She peered at him, his strong profile thrown into the shadows caused by the darkness and the illuminated control panel. She couldn't forget his eyes—like slate-gray storm clouds—that had locked on her face when he'd removed his goggles at the snow cave. One look and she'd known she would be all right.

"How long have I been asleep?"

"About an hour."

As snow and ice pelted the glass, she twisted around and stared out the window at the sky behind them. When she turned back, she saw some ground lights up ahead. "Anchorage?"

"Yes. The airport is closed to outgoing traffic but not to incoming. They have one runway they're keeping clear as much as possible. But the front end of the storm has already dumped a few inches on the area, with more to come."

A shudder rippled down Bree's body. "I hate to think how long I would have been at the wreck if you hadn't come to get me when you did." Then she remembered the men from the helicopter. "For some reason I don't think those guys who came when we left were there to rescue me or Jeremiah." She turned her full attention on David, whose square jaw was set in a firm line. "So why did they come?"

"I suppose they could have thought Jeremiah was carrying a cargo and intended to rob him."

"He brought some winter supplies to the village, but all he had in the cargo hold on the way back to Anchorage were two seals the Alaskan natives are allowed to hunt."

"And you."

"Yes. Jeremiah has flown me for the past—" A knot lodged in her throat making her voice raspy. She cleared it. "For the past couple of years since I became what I call an itinerant doctor. He told me when he started he did it because my dad would have wanted him looking out for me." Tears stung her eyes, and she blinked. A couple rolled down her cheeks. "I'm going to miss him. He lived next door to me, so we saw each other every day when we both were in town."

"Does he have any family? I've never heard him mention anyone but you. He was glad you were here in Alaska."

"No, my family was all he had." She barely choked out the last part as she thought of Christmas at the end of the month without Jeremiah. Without her parents, she realized she didn't have any immediate family close by anymore. "He and Dad were best friends from childhood. They both grew up here."

"So you've been living here all your life?" He looked toward her, and their gazes linked for a few seconds.

Bree stared into his gray eyes. In stark contrast to his black hair, eyebrows and lashes, their light color pulled her in and held her captive. Her mouth went dry, and her pulse rate spiked.

Finally he dragged his attention back to flying the plane, and she answered, "Except when I went to medical school. I returned to do my internship and residency here, though. Alaska is my home. I went to school in Oklahoma, where my mother's family lives. It sure was hot there. That's not for me. Even after four years I couldn't get used to the heat."

"Try the desert. I had several tours in places where temps rose to a hundred and twenty. That made me long for the time I spent stationed in Alaska. When I retired, I decided to come back and haven't regretted the decision."

"How long have you been here?"

"I was a pilot in the air force, and when I retired last year, I came back to Alaska. A good friend started Northern Frontier Search and Rescue and had to step down because of family obligations in the lower forty-eight. He asked me if I was interested in taking over. I wasn't sure, but after a few months shadowing him, I knew this was what I wanted to do."

She tried to remember what little she had heard about him from Jeremiah. At the moment all she could recall was the respect that Jeremiah had for David Stone. "Do you have family here?"

"No. My wife died and my daughter goes to college in California." He glanced at her.

"Although my dad is here for Christmas. He decided to come for the whole month."

David turned his concentration to landing the plane in the increasingly heavy winter storm. While he communicated with airport personnel, Bree tried to relax her body and not think of the last landing she'd experienced. But as the lights of the runway glowed through the falling snow, she couldn't stop thinking of Jeremiah and the change that had happened in a blink of an eye.

They'd been flying and then suddenly Jeremiah was in pain, barely able to hang on and land the plane. She needed to learn to fly, especially if she was going to continue to visit the villages.

After a bumpy descent, the Cessna touched down on the runway, and Bree held her breath as the plane slid and fishtailed. Tension whipped through her as the wind buffeted against the aircraft. David fought to keep it from going into the deeper snow on the side. She grasped the edge of the seat and prayed. She'd been doing a lot of that lately, but she knew God was the only one who could do anything when things went out of control.

David managed to avoid the snowdrift to the right and keep the plane on the runway. As he taxied toward a hangar at the small airport, he asked, "Are you okay?"

"Now I am. But I'm not eager to go for a flight anytime soon after the past few days."

"With everything in life there can be risk, but this was worth it. You're home safe now."

"Not quite, unless I can bum a ride with you or get a taxi. Jeremiah took me to the airport."

"Where do you live?"

She gave him the address. "It's on the outskirts of town. If that's too far—"

"Stop right there. I didn't fly out to rescue you only to leave you stranded at the airport. I live in that direction, only a few miles away from you. It's not out of the way."

When the Cessna was parked in the hangar, Bree finally felt safe. It had been a harrowing twenty-four hours she never wanted to repeat. Her body and mind screamed exhaustion, but she still had to get through the snow to her house before the street crews had a chance to clear the roads.

While David exited the plane, Bree did the same on her side, so glad to be standing on solid, dry land in the hangar. *Thank You, Lord. Now I hope You can bring Jeremiah home so I can lay him to rest.*

She knew that Jeremiah had made her executor of his estate, which as far as she knew was only his small house next to hers and the aircraft, but that was probably beyond repair. Her main concern was recovering his body and having a memorial service for his flying buddies. A lot of people would miss Jeremiah, especially her.

David rounded his Cessna with her duffel bag. "I need to make a couple of calls to the authorities and to my team to make sure everyone got word you're safe and they're all home safe, too."

"What about Jeremiah?" She wasn't even sure where to begin with making arrangements to recover his body.

As if he'd read her thoughts, he said, "I can help you make arrangements as soon as it's okay to return to the lake."

Relief trembled through her. "Thanks. I'd appreciate any help you can give me. I never thought I would have to do something like that. Since Jeremiah doesn't have any family, I'm it."

"Come sit in my office while I make the calls." He led her toward the hangar. "I've found that having the home base for the Northern Frontier Search and Rescue Organization is better near the airport. Saves time usually."

Inside there was a couch and a couple of comfortable chairs clustered together at the far end. A desk was situated near the door where they entered.

"Make yourself comfortable while I make

those calls." David gestured toward the black leather sofa.

"Is that where you work?" Bree pointed at the desk with a computer and printer on it as well as a stack of folders next to the phone. A filing cabinet sat under a large, very detailed map of Alaska showing the rivers, lakes, mountains and highway system.

"No, my assistant does. My office is through that door. Ella Jackson is the paid staff for the organization and has regular hours. She makes everything run smoothly. I'm glad, though, Ella did as I asked. She hates leaving when a search is going on, but I wanted her home before the storm moved through."

"You volunteer your time?" The more she was around David Stone, the more she wanted to learn about him. That thought surprised her because since her fiancé had died in a skiing accident six years ago she'd put her job first in her life. There were many people who needed a doctor, especially in certain parts of Alaska that were hard to access.

"Yes, except for Ella everyone is a volunteer. Maybe I can recruit you. We can always use medical personnel, especially with a big search."

She smiled. "I'm not above being persuaded."

"Good." His whole face lit up, his gray eyes

glittering. "My friends have learned to run the other way when they see me coming."

"Really?"

He laughed. "No. In fact, I've come to depend on them when I need people to help in a difficult search and rescue. They're so willing to give of their time. It makes me humble." He started for the closed door to his office. "Sit— put your feet up."

The soft black leather beckoned her, and Bree sank onto the couch. She spied the throw pillow at one end and pulled it to her. Laying her head on it, she stretched out and thought she would close her eyes for a few minutes until David was ready. She heard the murmur of his deep baritone voice coming from the office and settled farther into the cushion. His voice comforted her and gave her a feeling of safety. Sleep overtook her almost instantly.

"Thanks, Chance, for looking into this. Something went down at the rescue site after we left. Good thing we moved out when we did. I don't think those men were friendlies." As David talked to his friend, his hand clutched the phone tighter than he intended. He had to relax his grip before his fingers locked around the cold piece of plastic. "I've decided to go back in when it's clear to pick up Jeremiah's body."

"If I can, I'd like to go with you. In case there's trouble."

"I was hoping you'd volunteer."

Chance O'Malley, an Alaskan state trooper, chuckled. "Every time you call I seem to volunteer."

"I'm surprised I caught you at home. I thought you'd be out in this storm."

"I'm on duty in a couple of hours. Going in early. Lots of wrecks. Some people think just because they have a four-wheel-drive vehicle with snow tires, they can do anything."

David laughed. "You mean we can't?"

"I'd better not be pulling you out of a ditch. Get home. It's going to get worse before it gets better."

"Bye and thanks." David replaced the receiver and snatched up the keys to his Jeep.

When he stood, he stretched and rolled his head in a circle. Bree was probably pacing by now. His calls had taken longer than he'd anticipated, but everyone was back safely at their homes. He always liked to know that after a successful rescue. He never wanted to have to search for a searcher.

He entered the reception area and found Aubrey stretched out on his sofa asleep. Her long blond hair spilled over her shoulders like a waterfall caught in the golden rays of the sun. His gaze traveled down her petite body, then returned to her face. Her expression was peaceful, as though she hadn't nearly died the day before.

She saved lives, whereas he'd taken more than he wanted to count. For a few seconds, his final mission before he'd returned stateside and retired, wheedled its way into his thoughts. Faces of the men who had died under his command haunted his dreams, especially Lieutenant Adams. He squeezed his eyes closed, as though that would stop the images. His last tour in the Middle East had been one too many, leaving its mark on him more than all the others before it.

Bree stirred, her eyes slowly opening. They captured his and held him prisoner for a long moment before she averted her gaze and swung her legs to the floor to stand. "It's my turn to ask. Are you all right? Did you get some bad news?"

Only my memories. If only I could forget… "No. When the storm clears, I'm going to recover Jeremiah's body. I talked with my friend—Chance O'Malley—who will help me. He's a state trooper."

"I'm also going."

"You don't have to."

"Yes, I do. I owe Jeremiah my life."

"I understand, but—"

"Please. It's important. If I'm going to volunteer for Northern Frontier, then this should be no different." Although weary from her ordeal, she tilted up her chin and met his look with determination.

He shook his head, chuckling. "You're one tough lady. It's okay if you come. I thought it would be difficult for you to return to the scene of the wreck."

"I didn't say it wouldn't be, but I have to see this to the end. I want to know what those men were there for if they weren't part of the search and rescue."

"Me, too. When I talked with Chance, he said there haven't been any reports recently of people going to downed planes and robbing them before rescuers can reach them. But there were a few a couple of years ago."

"Like modern-day pirates? If that's what those guys were doing, they didn't get anything worth their time and trouble."

"Good thing I started out before dawn, or we might have met in the air."

Bree rubbed her hands up and down her sweater-clad arms. "Not a pretty thought, especially with the weapons they were carrying. God was looking out for us."

David picked up Aubrey's coat from the back of one of the chairs and handed it to her. "Let's go before we won't be able to leave here."

"Sounds good to me."

"That red Jeep in the hangar is mine." David followed her to his vehicle.

He started the engine and warmed the car up. After pushing the remote door opener, he slowly made his way into the heavy blowing snow to the road, and then drove toward Aubrey's house. With his full attention focused on the few feet in front of his SUV, the long ride was completed in silence.

When he turned onto her street, he glanced over at her. Her eyes were closed, her head resting on the window next to her. He smiled, glad his home wasn't far from hers. It had been a long day, and sleep lured him, as well.

He pulled into her driveway close to her front entrance, switched off his car and shifted toward her. "Aubrey, we're at your house."

Her eyes opened, and, as before in his office, they connected with his. Again he felt a bond with her, more than anyone else he'd ever rescued. The sensation surprised him, causing him to break their visual link. Keeping his emotions checked while rescuing a person always helped him do what needed to be done. But the second he'd seen Aubrey's brown eyes at the wreck site, something had changed. He must be more exhausted than he realized.

"Call me Bree. All my friends do."

Her soft voice floated to him, pulling him back to her. "Ready?"

"Yes, but you don't have to go with me. I can carry my duffel bag. No sense in you getting cold and wet. It's not like this is a date or anything." She reached behind her and pulled her bag over the seat. "Thank you. Please let me know when you'll be recovering Jeremiah's body. I have some downtime between assignments. I volunteer at a free clinic in Anchorage, but I can change my hours if need be."

He removed his wallet and withdrew a business card, then gave it to her. "Call if you need anything. My cell phone number is on there."

"Thank you. I hope in a few days I can repay you with dinner. I love to cook."

"Sure. Let me know when."

A blast of cold air and some snow swept inside when she opened the door and slid out of the SUV. He waited for her to round its front and make her way to her house. He might not walk her to her door, but he would at least stay until she was inside. When he looked out the side window, she still stood by the door, facing the house next door.

Is something wrong?

He climbed from his Jeep. "Bree?"

She peered back at him. "There's a light on in Jeremiah's house. I think someone is inside."

THREE

In the driving snow, David rounded the hood of his Jeep and stopped next to Bree. "He probably just left a light on."

Her teeth digging into her lower lip, Bree didn't have a good feeling about this. "No, Jeremiah never does. He doesn't like to waste electricity. There's a switch right by the door, so it's easy for him to come in and flip it on." She pointed toward the back of the house. "I think there's one on in the kitchen. I want to check to see. What if someone heard he was dead and came to rob him?"

"I know the news can spread fast when one of the bush pilots dies in a wreck, but someone would have to be crazy to do something like that, especially in a storm. There's no vehicle around, and I can't see the intruder escaping far on foot." He waved his hand toward the front. "And there are no footprints leading to the porch."

"How about around back?"

"What's behind your houses?"

"Woods."

"Which would make it hard to remove his valuable possessions that way and carry them through the trees to where they parked their car."

Maybe she was overreacting, but ever since those guys showed up at the wreck site, she'd been unsettled. "Okay, chalk it up to a curious, tired woman, but I'm still going to check. What if they came earlier and the new snow covered their tire tracks and footprints? It won't take much in this storm. Besides, he has a cat I need to bring over to my house. I know Ringo is used to being alone, but I still don't want to leave him by himself any longer."

"If you think there's someone in the house, then we should call the police."

"Who won't be able to come anytime soon. They have their hands full right now dealing with this storm. Maybe an intruder came the day before yesterday. Jeremiah flew to Daring then and stayed overnight before bringing me back. Like you pointed out, there isn't a vehicle around, so the person is probably gone, but what if they let Ringo out?"

"Then I'll go with you. Do you have a key?"

"Yes, in my house." Cold shivered down

her length, and she clasped her arms across her chest.

"In case something is going on at Jeremiah's, I'll stay out here and wait for you to get it. And if I see a cat, I'll grab it."

"You might not see Ringo. He's totally white and deaf so calling his name isn't useful. I'll be right back." Bree trudged toward her house, digging her key out of the front zipped pocket in her parka. Inside her place, she quickly went to the drawer in her desk and grabbed Jeremiah's key.

The warmth tempted her to stay, but she wouldn't. She needed to make sure Ringo was all right and bring him over. If she couldn't take care of Ringo because of her crazy schedule as an itinerant doctor, she'd make sure he had a home with a friend.

She joined David outside, and they plowed through the newly fallen snow to Jeremiah's porch, where the overhang and alcove protected them from the wind and storm. When David withdrew the handgun he'd had with him at the wreck site, the action hammered home the seriousness of what they were doing. She was glad he was there. After she unlocked the front door, he took the lead and entered Jeremiah's house.

She trailed behind him, hoping to see Ringo, who would greet her if he saw her. A few steps inside, she glimpsed the chaos in the living area off the entrance. Cushions from the couch and two chairs, as well as items from the drawers, littered the floor. She started to enter the room, but David put an arm up to stop her.

He mouthed the words, "Let me go first."

She nodded.

He went into the living room and searched any places a person could hide while Bree swung her attention between him and the hallway that led to the back of the house.

David returned to her side and whispered close to her ear, "It's clear and I can't tell if anything is taken, but definitely a person was looking for something. Which way is the kitchen?"

Looking for something? What? She waved her hand toward the dining room on the other side of the entry hall. "It leads to the kitchen, but so does this hallway."

"Stay here while I check the rest of the house. How many bedrooms?"

"Two and one bathroom. Look for Ringo." Worry nibbled at the edges of her mind. What was going on here? Jeremiah didn't have a lot. Most of his money had gone into his plane and the occasional vacation to Hawaii.

As David moved down the hallway and disappeared into the kitchen, Bree sidled into the living room and took in all the mess. It appeared as though the intruder had left nothing untouched. She didn't know everything that Jeremiah had, and it would take a while to go through the mess to see if she could tell if anything was missing. But what concerned her the most at the moment was Ringo. Jeremiah loved that cat.

She checked a couple of the feline's favorite spots in the living room. They were empty. What if he'd followed the intruder outside and was hunkered down somewhere trying to stay warm in the storm? What if the intruder took the cat or did something to Ringo?

Lord, please help me find Ringo. I don't—

A loud cry wafted to her from the hallway. *Ringo.* He was in the house. She knew that sound like a baby's whine. Hurrying into the small foyer, she hoped he would let out another belt. As David walked from the dining room, the cat protested and his paw appeared from beneath the coat closet door. She rushed to it and thrust it open. Ringo flew out of his prison, stopped halfway to the kitchen and noticed David, a stranger. The tomcat made a beeline to sniff him.

As Ringo rubbed himself against David's leg, putting his scent on him, he said, "It's all clear, but the rest of the house is like the living room—trashed. I called the police and reported the break-in. Since no one is in danger, they'll get to it tomorrow hopefully. Right now all officers are dealing with emergencies and the effects of the storm. I have a buddy who is a detective. I'll let him know what's going on, see if this is happening with other houses, especially in this area. I told them they would need to contact you. That you'll have a key to the place."

"Good. When I'm not so tired, I want to go through Jeremiah's house and see if I can tell if anything is missing. His big-screen TV is still here."

David's forehead scrunched as he frowned. "Too large to steal while a storm is dumping tons of snow on Anchorage?"

Bree shrugged. "You'd think a burglar would want it. It's only a couple of months old. Did you see how they got in?"

"Back door was jimmied."

"Is the lock broken?"

"Yes. I stepped out on the deck and noticed footprints leading away from the house, but the snow will fill them soon, even the ones on the covered stoop. Didn't see any coming to the house. They looked about the size of my boots. Twelve. I took a picture of them on my cell phone, although I don't know if that will help much."

"Only one set of footprints?"

"Yes, but like us earlier at the wreck site, one person could be using the other's footsteps. They weren't neat impressions. I'd usually say no one would be crazy enough to be out in this snowstorm, robbing people, but after what's happened here, anything is possible. There are some loose two-by-fours and a toolbox in the utility room. I could put them up across the door."

"I'd appreciate it if you would. I don't know when I can get a locksmith out here to change the lock."

David headed toward the kitchen with Ringo following. "I can do that for you. One of my hobbies is carpentry. When I'm not running Northern Frontier, I like to make pieces of furniture."

"You're a man of many talents."

When Bree came into the kitchen, the disarray, worse than the living room, stunned her. Torn boxes of food were emptied on the floor and counters. The refrigerator and freezer remained open; the contents had been gone through. Anger festered in the pit of her stomach. She curled and uncurled her hands.

David disappeared into the utility room. When he emerged with the boards and hammer, he stopped near her. "I haven't disturbed anything, but I think it's okay if you shut the freezer and refrigerator. The rest I think the police should see."

She turned toward him. His image blurred as tears flooded her eyes. She'd been trying not to think of what had happened over the past twenty-four hours, but suddenly it all crashed down on her.

David leaned the wood against the table and put the hammer and nails on it, and then he enveloped her in an embrace. "I'm sorry this happened on top of everything else. It's hard to take in."

"He was family to me. He was always here if I needed something. I…" Her mind went blank with grief. Numb, she couldn't even express how she was feeling.

His arms tightened about her as she cried against him. For a few moments, she didn't feel so alone. Jeremiah was her last tie to her parents. In the past years she'd gone through three losses: first her dad, then her fiancé and finally her mom. And now Jeremiah. Death surrounded her, even in her job. Everyone she loved died. Suddenly it seemed too much to bear. Tears continued to flow from the depth of her soul, and the whole time David sheltered her, his hand stroking her back.

Slowly she pulled herself together. She never fell apart in front of people, especially someone she'd just met. She stepped away, swiping her fingers across her face. "I don't usually do that. As a doctor, I've seen my share of death."

"Having served in several war zones, so have I, but you never get used to it. With my last tour of duty, all that death started really getting to me that I couldn't do my job the way I should. I knew then I had to retire."

"And now you're heading a search and rescue organization. That doesn't seem like you're getting away from death."

"A lot of the times we find people alive. That makes up for the ones we can't reach in time. I feel like I'm making a difference, doing something positive."

"But you didn't while serving?" Although she'd seen death as a doctor, more often she was able to help someone heal.

"There's little positive about war. I saw a lot of destruction. A man can only see so much before it starts changing him."

Bree swallowed at the pain echoing in his voice. A shutter fell over his features. Did something happen to him during that last tour of duty? She knew some veterans who had served in war zones and most were silent about their experiences.

The urge to comfort him, as he did her, compelled her forward. She reached out, clasping his hand. "When I can't help a patient anymore and have to stand back and watch them die, I put them in God's hands. There comes a time when only He can do anything. Jeremiah is with Him now, and that does console me."

David's chest rose and fell with a deep breath. "I'd better get this door fixed so you can go to sleep and I can go home."

Bree watched David nail the two-by-fours across the door frame. With his coat off, she admired his well-proportioned build. She could see him working with wood to create a piece of furniture. He'd said he'd served twenty years in the air force, so she guessed he might be around forty. He was attractive with strong features, a small cleft in his chin and short black hair. But what really caught her attention were his smoky-gray eyes, like the clouds as a storm moved in.

He glanced over his shoulder at her and gave her a lopsided smile. Caught staring at him, she looked away. Her gaze fixed on the mess.

She hated standing in the middle of the chaos; she wanted to clean up. She hoped the police found some evidence pointing to who had done this. Coupled with the guys at the lake, she couldn't shake the feeling that something nefarious was going on. Jeremiah lived a quiet life, spending time with her when she was in town or with his small group of friends, mostly pilots and outdoorsmen.

"I'm through. If someone really wants to, he could get in, but that's true of most places unless there's high security." David walked into the utility room and put up the hammer.

Bree looked again at what some determined person had done to Jeremiah's house, as though he was searching for something. But what? The most expensive item Jeremiah had in his home was the TV. A shudder rippled down her spine. "What's going on here?"

"I suppose it could have been teens trashing a place for fun. Did Jeremiah have a run-in with a teen lately?"

"I don't know. I've been gone for a month. When I talked with him, he didn't mention any problems. In fact, he was upbeat as if everything was going great. He didn't say anything about feeling bad, either. I know heart attacks can strike suddenly, but sometimes there are signs." She remembered her conversation with Jeremiah right before he had his heart attack. "Of course, I might be the last person he would say anything to. He thought I was a mother hen when it came to his health."

"You see what happens when people don't take care of themselves. Ready to go?"

"Just a moment. I need to get the cat food,

litter box and Ringo. He's going home with me."
Bree found the carrier in the utility room as well
as the food. "The litter box is in the bathroom."

"Yeah, all over the place like everything else."

Bree checked the floor by the washing ma-
chine and spied a twenty-pound bag of litter.
While she grabbed a liner, she asked, "Can you
get the empty box? I'll fix up a fresh one at my
place."

After gathering the items she needed and
Ringo, she left a couple of lights on to give
the illusion someone was at home. When she
stepped out into the driving snow, she tramped
toward her house with David right behind her,
carrying the box with the litter and food bags
in it.

Inside the warmth of her place, she released
Ringo, who shot out of the carrier and raced up
the staircase. "He likes to lie on my coverlet."

"Can I help you with any of this?"

She swept around and took his load from his
arms. "You need to go home. The roads are getting worse by the minute."

"Yes, ma'am. I can tell you're used to giving orders." He winked and strolled to the front
door. "I'll call you tomorrow, but feel free to call
me if you need something."

"I'll be fine," she said with more bravado than

she felt. "Thanks for all you did for me. I could have died today."

A smile spread across his face. "Anytime. Today is the good part of my job."

After he left, Bree turned the lock. Its clicking sound shouted to her that she was alone with a deaf cat as a companion, and there was a burglar out there who had ransacked her neighbor's home.

David arrived home thirty minutes later after creeping through the streets. The only good thing was that he hadn't encountered a lot of traffic because of the storm and late hour. He parked in his garage, hooked up his battery to keep it charged and then made his way into his kitchen.

His dad came into the room from the hallway. "I heard the garage door. How did it go? Any problems taking the doctor home?"

"Other than a nasty night out there, no. But there was a problem when we arrived at her house. Jeremiah Elliot's house was broken into. He lived next door to her. She saw a light on and insisted on investigating it. The place was completely trashed but nothing obvious was taken." David went on to mention some of the more valuable items of Jeremiah's that were still there.

His father's eyes sparked with interest. "How did they get in?"

"They?"

"That much damage often implies more than one person."

Since his dad had recently retired as a police chief of a medium-size town in Colorado, he would know. "Through the back door. Jeremiah's house was not a fortress. The lock wasn't a good one."

"Most burglars want to hit a place fast and get out quick. It sounds like they were looking for something in particular, or it may have been mischief-making teens."

"Jeremiah's death wasn't common knowledge. I reported it to the authorities, but until they checked for next of kin, they were going to keep his death quiet." Although Bree had said Jeremiah didn't have any next of kin, there was a possibility she wasn't aware of a long-lost relative.

"Then something else might be going on here." His dad ambled to the sink, filled a glass with water and took his nightly pills. "Growing old isn't for the faint of heart."

"You miss your job?"

"Yes. It's been six months, and I don't know what to do with myself. If I'd had my way, I would still be police chief."

David knew the PD had a ceiling on how old a person could be to serve.

"Just because you retired from one job doesn't mean you can't do something else," he told his father.

"Nothing else appeals to me."

"A security consultant?"

"I'd rather do something different. That way I won't yearn for a job I can't have anymore. There's nothing in Colorado for me."

David had been ready to leave the service after twenty years. Now, at forty-one, he was enjoying what he was doing, and he wasn't financially dependent on a paycheck because of his pension and some wise investments over the years. He could do what he really wanted. "Is that why you decided to come for the whole month of December?"

"There's no one in Colorado, not even your daughter since she started college. I saw Melissa at Thanksgiving when she and some friends came to ski, otherwise she has been a stranger. I miss her. When is she coming for Christmas?"

"A few days before." She was only coming because her grandfather would be there. Otherwise David wouldn't have seen her at all. Ever since his wife had died three years ago, and David had had to go overseas for his last tour of duty, Melissa had lived with his father.

His father's dark bushy eyebrows crunched into a single line. "Why not sooner?"

"You know Melissa and I haven't been on the best of terms since Trish died. She blames me for her mother's death."

"You weren't responsible for that, and I've made that clear to Melissa."

"Dad, I wasn't there when Trish needed me."

"Because you were serving your country."

Tension gripped David as he thought back to three years ago when Trish had taken a lethal combination of alcohol and painkillers. He'd been halfway around the world, supporting ground troops as a B-52 pilot. Earlier, when he'd left Trish after her operation to repair her damaged knee and returned to the war zone, she'd been improving—or so she said—and had urged him to leave. If only he'd known then that she'd become dependent on painkillers, maybe she would be alive today.

"Son, stop blaming yourself. You can't change the past. Focus on the here and now."

"I'm trying."

"Is that why you're working so hard when you're supposed to be retired? You've made some good investments. You don't even have to work, but then your job at the search and rescue organization is strictly volunteer."

"I'm only forty-one. Just because I retired

from the service doesn't mean I'm going to lie around on some beach doing nothing."

His father chuckled. "Well, certainly not here in Alaska. But Hawaii is only a plane ride away."

Too wired, David prowled around his kitchen, needing to sleep but not sure he could, even after his previous night sleeping restlessly on the couch in his office. "This volunteer job is perfect for me. I'd go crazy without it. You of all people should know what that feels like."

His dad held up his hands as if in surrender. "Okay. You've made your point. The Stone men aren't good at relaxation."

David started to reply when his cell phone rang, jolting him. As he answered it, he glimpsed Chance's name on the screen.

"I hope I didn't wake you," his friend said.

"No, Dad and I were talking. What's up?"

"I did some checking after we talked earlier, and I thought you might like to know Jeremiah's emergency locator transmitter hasn't sent a signal since the last pass of the satellite. I know you didn't turn it off, since you were back in Anchorage by then, so who did?"

FOUR

The hairs on David's nape tingled. He looked toward his dad as he answered Chance. "I don't know. I called off the search and rescue teams on the ground. From what I understand, they were safe and back before the storm got too bad. They never made it to the site. How is the weather near the wreck?"

"It moved through there fast, so the weather at the site has improved in the past couple of hours."

David thought about the white helicopter with the heavily armed men, and an alarm clanged against his skull. His gut tightened. He didn't have a good feeling about this situation, especially with the break-in at Jeremiah's.

"I was hoping that you'd tell me a ground rescue team made it to the wreck." Chance's comments pulled David back to the conversation.

"I suppose the transmitter could have malfunctioned after sending a signal for a while, but this makes me wonder if the men in the helicopter had anything to do with the ELT not working."

"Good question. One we might be able to answer when we return to pick up Jeremiah's body."

"I think we need to go as soon as the conditions permit us." From years serving in combat, an urgency nipped at David. He couldn't shake the feeling something was very wrong with the situation—one Bree was involved in.

After David hung up, he stared at his cell phone, the urge strong to call Bree and make sure she was all right. He glanced at his watch and noticed it had been an hour since he'd left her. She was probably in bed, and he hated to wake her up after the past twenty-four hours she'd endured, but he'd be at her house first thing in the morning if he had to cross-country ski to get there.

"Something wrong, son?"

David walked to the window in the breakfast nook and peeked out the blinds at the snowstorm still raging. He couldn't see the trees in his backyard. "I don't know. I'm probably overreacting, but the emergency locator transmitter isn't sending out a signal in Jeremiah's plane anymore. It was working fine earlier. I didn't turn it off at the wreck site." David twisted toward his dad and told him about the helicopter and the armed men.

His forehead wrinkled, his father pushed away from the counter, his body stiff. "I don't like this. You know how I feel about coincidences. What if Jeremiah didn't have a heart attack? What if he was poisoned or something else that could look like a heart attack?"

A chill swept through David. As a police officer, his dad had seen so much evil in his job. Could Jeremiah have been poisoned? "Murdered? Why?"

"I don't know, but if I were you, I would have Chance look into it."

"We'll retrieve his body as soon as we can, and hopefully that'll tell us what killed him." David released a deep breath. Exhaustion clung to him. "I think I'll call Bree and make sure she's okay."

"Are you going to tell her about the transmitter?"

"I don't want her worrying unnecessarily. I'll do enough for the both of us." He turned back to the window and lifted the blinds. The driving snow still obscured his view. "If I can't get over to see her, I don't think anyone else can, either." At least he hoped that was the case.

Lord, I need You to watch out for Bree. The prayer came unbidden into his mind. He'd prayed other ones in the past that had gone unanswered. Would this one?

"I'm going to bed. If you need me, I'm here for you. Although I don't think you're going anywhere for a while." His dad nodded toward the blizzard conditions outside the window.

David sank into the chair at the table and called Bree. He *needed* to hear her voice, then maybe he could get some sleep. When she answered, he sagged with relief. "This is David. I hope I didn't wake you up."

"No, I finished settling Ringo into my house and putting things away. I'm tired but not sleepy. I thought I would come home and go directly to sleep, but I can't stop thinking about what has happened, especially the break-in."

"Do you want me to come over and keep you company?" he asked before really thinking through how he would manage that.

Bree chuckled. "Have you looked outside lately? Do you think anyone is going anywhere right now?"

"No, but…" *What? I'm worried someone killed Jeremiah, and you're possibly in danger?* "I don't know what I was thinking. I doubt I could find my way even on my cross-country skis. The good news is I've heard the system is moving fast, so maybe it won't be too bad by morning."

"I hope not. I have a ton of stuff to do." Her voice softened. "But I imagine it'll be a while before the streets will be cleared."

"I'll let you go. We both need some sleep, but if you need anything, call me. I'll see what I can do, blizzard or not."

"Thanks, but you've already rescued me once today."

"Hey, remember I'm the head of a SAR group. That's my job."

After hanging up with Bree, David stood and closed the blind he'd opened. When he lay down a few minutes later, as much as he wanted to relax and sleep, his mind raced with all that had happened earlier. This was what came from having a cop for a father. He began to imagine all the bad possibilities surrounding Jeremiah's death. He turned onto his side and pounded his fist into his pillow.

Everyone had loved Jeremiah, he told himself. No one wanted to harm him. And Bree was a doctor. She knew what a heart attack looked like.

But the thoughts didn't appease him. Only seeing Bree tomorrow would do that.

The first thing Bree saw when she awakened the next morning was Ringo standing over her in bed, whining. He missed Jeremiah. Sitting up, Bree cuddled the white cat and scratched behind his ears. "I know. You don't understand why you're here and not at home. You're stuck with me for the time being." At least until she found him a new family.

She hated thinking about that. If only she could take care of him, but she was gone for a month at a time with her job. Giving him one final hug, she scooted to the edge of her bed and rose, then put Ringo on the floor. He ambled out of the room while Bree walked to the window to see if the snow had stopped yet.

White greeted her everywhere she looked. Probably an additional foot to the five or six inches that had been already on the ground. And the street out front was still packed with snow. It might be a day or so before it was cleared. Good thing she wasn't expected at the clinic right away.

But she needed to see to Jeremiah's house. She had a friend who was a police officer. She'd check with her later today about the report she and David made last night. She headed to the closet to pick out something to wear.

David. What would she have done if he hadn't reached her at the wreck site when he had? A shudder snaked down her spine when she thought about the men in white. She would have flagged them down, thinking they were there to help her. Now she didn't think they had been.

Five minutes later, Bree entered her kitchen and made a pot of coffee, the whole while thinking about David. After he'd called last night, she'd actually been able to sleep for an hour or two before her memories of the ordeal intruded again. There was someone who cared. She felt as if she had a comrade in this situation—whatever that was. As a doctor, she searched for answers to what was wrong with her patients. She didn't give up until she had a solution, but she was out of her element with armed men and a break-in.

After pouring a mug full of coffee, she strolled toward her living room. The sound of a snowmobile disturbed the quiet. She opened the blinds to see a man dressed in black pull up close to her house. She stiffened, her hand clenching the mug. Taking a step back from the window, she tried to remember where her ammo and bear gun were. The hall closet where she'd put it after her hiking expedition last summer, she remembered.

The man started for her porch, fidgeting with the strap under his chin. She placed her cup on the table nearby and was turning to make a run for the hallway when he removed the helmet.

David. Her tension melted as her shoulders

dropped. Weak with relief, she took a few seconds to compose herself. She was more rattled than she'd realized.

The chimes of the doorbell filled the house before she finally moved toward the hallway. She greeted David with a smile. "I can't believe you're here. Come in." Stepping to the side, she drank in the sight of him. His presence comforted her. "Would you like some coffee? You've got to be freezing."

He removed his thick gloves, then began unzipping his parka. "Not too bad. I thought about skiing here, but this was quicker."

"Let's go into the kitchen. Have you had breakfast yet?"

"I grabbed an egg and bacon sandwich but I could always eat more."

"Well, I can't profess to be a great cook, but I can manage a decent breakfast." Bree made her way toward her kitchen. She was glad to see him. Last night she'd fought with the covers and they had won. Although technically she'd slept, she didn't feel rested. She dreamed about the wreck, the break-in at Jeremiah's. David being here now gave her solace and soothed her apprehension.

After pouring a mug of coffee for David, she opened the refrigerator and noticed the items that Jeremiah had stocked for her as he always did the day before she returned home from a village. Tears jammed her throat and glistened in her eyes. It was one of the many things he'd done for her over the years.

"Bree?"

David's deep baritone penetrated her sorrow, drawing her back to the moment. "Thanks to Jeremiah, I have eggs, milk, cheese. Do you want an omelet?" Her words held no inflection, as if she were on autopilot.

David came up behind her, close but not touching. "I'll eat whatever you want. I can even help you."

She shook away her last picture of Jeremiah slumped in the cockpit and removed the carton of eggs. "No, you're my guest, and, besides, I need to do something."

"I'm sorry. I know how important Jeremiah was to you. I'm a good listener."

"I'm not ready." She withdrew the milk, cheese and bacon. "I think I'm still numb."

"I understand. It's been just barely two days. My offer still stands when you're ready. Loss is part of life but so hard on the living."

Amen to that. With Jeremiah's death, she should know, having lost everyone she had been close to. There were no adequate words.

"I appreciate the offer. Right now I'm going to focus on fixing breakfast, then making a call to the police to see when they will investigate the break-in."

"I can do that while you're cooking. I know several high-ranking police officers. That's one of the perks of heading a search and rescue organization."

"Great. Is there anything you can do about getting my street cleared soon?"

David laughed. "I wish I had that kind of pull. But if you need a ride somewhere, I have room on my snowmobile."

"No, I'm fine today and tomorrow. I'll use the time to clean up Jeremiah's house. But I'm due at the clinic after that." Bree cracked an egg and dumped it into a bowl.

"It's okay if you take time off."

She threw him a glance over her shoulder. "This coming from a man I suspect doesn't take a lot of time off. You're a full-time volunteer with a carpentry job on the side."

He pulled out his cell phone. "Okay. I admit I'm a workaholic."

While David called his friend at the police station, Bree cooked the bacon in the microwave, then crumbled the bits in the omelets she prepared. He wrapped up his conversation as she brought the food to the table. Bree went back and picked up the coffeepot, refilled their mugs and took a seat across from David.

"This smells wonderful." He stuffed his cell phone in his pocket.

She thanked him, then bowed her head in prayer. "Lord, please give Jeremiah a hug for me. Bless this food and the man across from me. He saved my life." When she looked up, she found David staring at her, his expression thoughtful.

"I was doing my job." He dropped his gaze to his omelet. "That's all."

"One I'm grateful for. What did your friend say?" Bree slipped her first bite into her mouth.

"The streets aren't clear, but as a favor to me, he'll come out at the end of his shift and make out a report. Not one of his usual duties since he is a lieutenant and a detective."

"When?"

"Around twelve. He's been on duty all night." David took a swallow of his coffee. "I thought I would stay and help clear your sidewalk and driveway."

"I wish I could afford a heated driveway, but I have college loans to pay off."

"I have one. Definitely a nice convenience. But today you have me to help."

He gave her a smile that warmed her insides and began to thaw the numbness encasing her from the past forty hours. "Nor do I have a snowmobile, but I have skied to work."

"As soon as the airport runways are cleared, I'm flying to the wreck site. Thankfully I have the coordinates because the emergency locator transmitter isn't working anymore."

"It isn't? I never turned it off. I wonder if those men did."

David washed a bite of omelet down with another swig of coffee. "No, it was working when we returned to Anchorage."

"But not now. What does that mean?"

"I don't know. Probably nothing other than it was damaged and possibly malfunctioned."

Bree studied his face, void of emotion as though he were deliberately hiding what he really thought. "You think it's something else, don't you?"

"Someone might have come along and turned it off. It was working until the storm moved out of the area."

"A rescue team?"

"No, everyone was called off when I found you."

"I'm coming with you. Do you think we can go tomorrow? I'll feel better when we recover Jeremiah's body and give him a proper funeral. There are enough unanswered questions. With that resolved, it will be easier to move forward."

"Usually the airport clears at least one runway pretty fast since airplanes are one of the main modes of transportation in Alaska."

Bree finished the last of her omelet. As she stood to take her dishes over to the sink, David did, too. "I'll clean these up later. I'll go get my bunny boots."

"I'll take care of this while you get ready. That's the least I can do."

She gave him a smile. "A man who does dishes. How about windows?"

He chuckled. "Nope." He shooed her away. "Go on, so when the detective shows up we'll be through. I know the snow has covered any evidence of which way the intruder left after ransacking Jeremiah's place. After we look through the house, I want to go out back and check the directions the footsteps were headed yesterday. Who knows? We might find something."

"You are an optimistic guy."

"That's part of my job. I'm always optimistic that I *will* find the person I'm looking for."

"Even when it seems hopeless?"

"Yes, because that way I'm giving one hundred percent to the search."

Bree paused by the doorway. "That's the way I am when dealing with my patients. I'm determined they're going to get better."

Across the expanse of her kitchen, their gazes

linked, and the light in his gray eyes reached deep inside her, pushing the darkness away.

He smiled. "I'll meet you in the foyer in five minutes."

As Bree made her way to her bedroom, she thought about that last look. It almost made her forget about all the people she had been close to in the past years who had died. But she couldn't. She had to keep them front and center in her mind. She didn't want any more heartache. What she needed was more days at the free clinic. To throw herself even more into her job and forget all about the hope she'd felt looking into David's eyes.

David and Bree met the detective on Jeremiah's front porch. The tired lines on his friend's face spoke of a long night, probably dealing with one crisis after another. "Thanks for coming. Bree, this is Lieutenant Thomas Caldwell. Thomas, Dr. Bree Mathison."

After they shook hand, David continued, "Now that the introductions are over, we can get down to business. We haven't been inside since last night when we discovered the house had been broken into. As I told you, Jeremiah is dead and Bree is the executor of his will."

Thomas turned to Bree. "Do you think you

can go through the house and tell me if anything has been stolen?"

"If he bought something in the past month, no. Otherwise, maybe."

"Better than nothing." Thomas indicated that Bree should unlock the door.

When David stepped into the house, he was hit all over again with how thorough whoever trashed the place had been. He couldn't see anything not searched. "This isn't the work of a teenage prank. Too organized."

"I agree." Thomas moved to the living room. "I've been to crime scenes which turned out to be some teenagers looking for a kick. In this case, I think someone was looking for something specific." He flipped his hand toward the bookcase. "Every book has been checked, then tossed into that pile."

"Jeremiah didn't have a lot," Bree said. "All his money went into his plane and recently the TV, but it's still here." She made a full circle of the room. "I forgot how bad this is. I'm not even sure where to begin."

Thomas started taking photographs. "I'll walk through the house. If I have any questions, I'll give a holler."

David took hold of Bree's hand, now minus the gloves she'd stuffed in her parka's pockets.

He rubbed her hands between his palms. "We'll take it one room at a time. I'll help."

"You've got an organization to run."

"Ella can keep me informed. This is too big a job for one person. I might also be able to talk my dad into helping."

"That's right. He's visiting you. I hate to take you away from him."

"You aren't. I'm volunteering, and I know my dad. He will, too."

Her eyes shiny, she blinked and averted her face while she swiped her free hand across her cheeks.

He gently squeezed the one he still held. "Like this cleanup, one step at a time. One day at a time."

She swung her attention back to his face. "Jeremiah's gone. I still can't believe it. I…" She swallowed hard.

Thomas came back into the living room. "Does Jeremiah have a computer? I couldn't find one."

"Not a big one, just a tablet. He usually kept it in his bedroom. He loves—loved to read books on it before going to bed. I gave it to him for his birthday because the print was getting too small for him in books. It isn't on his bedside table?" Bree's words rushed together as if she couldn't get them out quickly enough.

"I didn't see one."

With her eyes wide and glistening, Bree charged past Thomas.

David exchanged a look with Thomas. "I'll go see about her. This has hit her hard."

"I understand. This house is worse than most I've seen searched. I'll be in the kitchen. I want to check the back door and the area around it since you said that was the entry point."

David headed down the short hallway to Jeremiah's bedroom and found Bree on her hands and knees, looking under the bed. She sat back on her heels and peered up at him.

"It's not here. Why would someone take a tablet worth a few hundred dollars and leave this?" Bree gestured toward the wall mount with a shotgun and rifle still on it. When she rose to her feet, she held a revolver. "This is brand-new. Jeremiah had a small collection of guns that he kept under his bed. I didn't think about those guns last night since the shotgun and rifle were still in place. The other three handguns are there, too. I know the TV is large and hard to conceal while carrying it away from here, but these weapons are easy and on the black market they would bring someone a nice stash of money." She panned the room. "He was always helping others. I don't understand…" Her last sentence ended on a sob.

David came to her and took the Glock from her hand, then placed it on the bedside table. "Sometimes there is no rhyme or reason to things that occur."

She hugged her arms against her chest, one tear then another sliding down her cheeks. "I've worked ER. I should be used to what people do to others."

David framed Bree's face, touched by the sorrow in her expression. All he wanted to do was take the pain away. The pads of his thumbs wiped away her tears as they flowed unchecked. Finally he drew her against him and enclosed her in his embrace. She cried, the sound solidifying his need to help her get to the bottom of what was going on. Maybe it was nothing. He hoped that was the case.

As he stroked her back, she cuddled even closer, her tears slowing until she finally leaned away and tilted her head back. "Thank you. I've needed to do that since the crash. All I could do last night was go over and over the wreck and wonder if there was anything I could have done to prevent Jeremiah's death. Everything happened so fast. I couldn't fly the plane, but even if I could, I don't know how I could have changed seats with him in time. I certainly couldn't do CPR. I couldn't—"

"Shh. I know it's human nature to look at a

situation and rehash it in your mind, trying to come up with a different ending. Sometimes there's nothing you can do to change the outcome. Don't beat yourself up over it. I know Jeremiah wouldn't want you to."

Now if only David could follow his own advice. He had many regrets—a few big ones that he hadn't been able to get past.

"You're right." She blew out a long sigh. "He would be the first to say regrets are a waste of time. The past is just that." She stepped away from him, rubbing her hand over her face. "Where's your friend?"

"In the kitchen, checking where the person or persons came in. I think whoever did this had help."

"They could have been here a long time. Probably were, to do this." Bree swept her arm across her body, then maneuvered around a pile of clothes pulled out from the dresser. She shook her head. "Jeremiah was always so neat. I'm glad he didn't see this."

"I wonder if any of your neighbors saw anything."

Bree halted in the doorway into the bedroom. "Maybe. There's no one near behind us, but Mr. and Mrs. Jefferson live across the street. They're retired. After Thomas leaves, we could go over there and talk to them."

"Go where?" Thomas's question came from the hallway. He approached Bree. "You two aren't going to investigate, are you?"

Bree's face reddened as she slanted a look over her shoulder. "I figure this isn't going to be a priority case, even with you being David's friend and the fact the tablet was stolen."

"I have to admit we have more pressing cases, but have you thought of something that might help?"

"Only questioning the few neighbors there are." David followed Bree from the room and paused in the hallway near Thomas.

"I'll do that, and I promise if I discover anything, I'll let you know. In fact, I'll do that right now. It's too bad we got so much snow last night. Any footprints you saw then are gone, but I'm sure you expected that."

"Am I free to start cleaning this up?" Bree asked as she started down the corridor.

"Yes. Let me know if you find the tablet anywhere in this mess or if something else is missing." Thomas pulled out a business card and passed it to Bree in the foyer.

She stuck it in her front pocket. "I appreciate you coming, especially today."

He shrugged. "Snow happens here. We can't let it stop everything."

David opened the front door, a chill sweeping into the house, and shook Thomas's hand. "Thanks. We'll be going to pick up Jeremiah's body tomorrow unless we have another storm system moving through."

"You and Bree?"

"And Chance O'Malley with the state police."

Thomas nodded. "Good. If I need to know something, you have my number."

David shut the door, then turned toward Bree. His gaze linked with hers, and the wall around his heart began to crumble. For the past three years, he'd shut down his emotions. That was the only way he could have functioned the last months of service. So much death and nothing he could do about it.

Bree looked toward the living room. "I guess I'll start in here. You don't have to stay. You've already helped me enough."

David ignored her and followed her into the living room. "You can't get rid of me that easily." There was no way he would leave her alone to deal with this. What if the people returned to look again?

The next day as the sun began its ascent in the eastern sky, Bree stared out the Cessna's window at the snow-blanketed ground below. The nearer she came to the wreck site, the tenser she became. Her clasped hands in her lap ached as she squeezed them tighter. Sweat beaded her forehead and upper lip.

Why did I insist on coming?

Because she owed Jeremiah for all the times he was there for her. Recovering his body had become important to her. The final act of kindness she could do for him.

"How much farther?" Chance asked, his husky voice coming through Bree's headset.

She glanced at him in the seat behind her. She'd met David's state trooper friend that morning and felt better that he was coming along. When she saw that both David and Chance were armed with not only a rifle but a revolver, too, flashes of the scene of those men dressed in white descending on the plane played through her mind. And she couldn't shake the feeling of danger.

"We're close. I'll fly over and assess where to land. I might use the same clearing as before. I know I can land safely there." David slid a look toward Bree as though asking her if that was okay.

She gave him a nod. He smiled, then returned his attention to flying. But the effects of his smile stayed with Bree. It comforted her and eased her anxiety.

Until the lake came into view. Bree sat forward,

staring out the windshield at the scene below. She searched the shoreline for the wreck and gasped. "The plane's gone."

FIVE

An hour later at the wreck site, Bree crested the rise, not far from where she'd made her snow cave, and saw an expanse of white interspersed with trees. No evidence of where she'd spent a terrifying night with wolves nearby.

Carrying a long pole, David came up beside her on the right. "Your duffel bag isn't where I dropped it."

Chance, with a rifle in his hands, took up a position on her left. "Are you sure of its location?"

"Yes. I memorized the exact cluster of trees so we could find it." He held up the pole. "I used this to poke holes all over the area, even out of range of where I thought it was." His gaze on the empty site below them, David frowned. "The shoreline has been disturbed, so we know we're in the right place. But there's no plane."

"Could it have sunk into the water?"

"Maybe. We know it didn't fly out of here,

which means either it is under the water or someone airlifted it."

Chance raised a set of binoculars to his eyes and surveyed the wreck site. "Let's go down and check it out. There are footprints near the area, but I don't see where they came from, so there's a possibility the helicopter returned and took the plane."

"Why would someone go to the trouble and expense?" David asked as he began his trek down the slope, using the pole to check the path ahead.

Still stunned, Bree automatically fell into step behind David with Chance following.

"After what you saw two days ago, if someone took the plane, they were most likely searching for something," Chance said. "So the question becomes, what? What was on the plane that someone would go to those lengths?"

"Besides some of the stuff I took with me to the village and an overnight bag for Jeremiah, the only cargo was the two seals." At the bottom of the incline, Bree stopped and turned around. "What are you implying?"

Chance stared right at her. "Something valuable. Something possibly illegal."

She squeezed her gloved hands into fists. "What? Drugs? There's no way Jeremiah would traffic in drugs knowingly. I suppose the seals could have drugs in them. You'll need to talk to the man who shipped them to Anchorage from Daring." The presence of David inches behind her quieted some of her anger at the state trooper for implying Jeremiah was a drug runner.

Chance frowned. "It's my job to look at all aspects of a case. I knew Jeremiah, and I agree with you, Bree, but I still have to consider it and rule it out. I will contact the man in Daring."

She drew in a frigid breath of air, trying to calm her heartbeat. "He hated taking medicine, even aspirin."

David placed his hand on her shoulder. "Which means he wouldn't take the drugs, but some dealers don't. They're in it for the money."

Bree whirled around and glared at David. His arms fell to his sides. "You, too?"

"Do you want to know what happened and why?"

The pounding of her heart against her rib cage clamored in her mind. "Yes, but why did you and Chance jump to that first?"

David sighed and clasped both of her upper arms. "Because drugs are a major problem here, as in other places. There's a lot of wilderness to cover in Alaska. And there is still the possibility of him not knowing he was transporting it."

"He had a heart attack, and suddenly we're

talking about him being a drug dealer." The heat of her anger kept the cold at bay. She had to make David and Chance realize that Jeremiah wouldn't do anything illegal. He had always been there for her. She would be there for him now.

"But we don't know what caused the heart attack. What if it was poison or something else?" David asked as Chance trudged toward the wreck site.

Bree glanced at the state trooper, then at David. Her vision blurred as tears filled her eyes. But she would not cry in front of him, having done enough of that yesterday. She was thankful her sunglasses shielded her eyes. "He was overweight and wouldn't take his blood pressure pills. Those two things could cause a heart attack."

"C'mon. Let's go check it out." But before David started, he turned to her. "I cared about Jeremiah, too, Bree. Like I told you, he was always ready to help me search by air if someone was missing."

"Yeah, right. Does that sound like a drug dealer?"

"I'm not saying he is. Neither is Chance. But everything has to be considered."

Bree sidestepped David and plowed ahead through the deep snow, glad she'd worn snowshoes. She paused next to Chance a few feet from the footprints that disturbed the pristine white landscape—that and the hole in the ice where the tail of the plane had been. New ice was already forming over the gap.

"The hole is too small for the plane to have sunk below the water," Bree finally broke the silence as all three of them took in the multiple footsteps.

"There probably were at least two or three people on the ground." Chance took several pictures before he went closer.

"If someone wanted the plane for whatever reason, then what did they do with Jeremiah's body?" Bree asked.

David pointed to one set of footsteps that headed into the nearby trees. "I'm going to see where these lead. Maybe one person walked in, although without snowshoes, that would be hard."

Chance studied the footprints, as if trying to determine how many sets there were. Bree felt useless doing nothing, so she trailed David.

He slowed his pace and waited for her. "Are you okay?"

"No, but I will be just as soon as everyone realizes Jeremiah is innocent."

David ducked down beneath the heavy drape of snow-encrusted evergreen branches and held them for Bree, who went into the stand of trees before him. She froze. Not far away the trail led to a mound of black on the ground—black like Jeremiah's outer winter clothing. She hurried toward the shape, praying it was her friend's body. Then at least she would be able to put him to rest.

When she reached what was a body, she knelt by it and rolled the frozen person toward her. Jeremiah. *Thank You, God. Now I can bury him.*

Although she'd seen her share of dead patients, she couldn't look at Jeremiah any longer than to ID him. She quickly rose and pivoted away while David approached. "It's him."

"I guess whoever took the plane didn't want a dead body in it."

"Why did the person bring him here?"

"Didn't want anyone from the air seeing a body on the ground, I'd guess. Black is hard to miss when everything else is white. The trees block an aerial view of Jeremiah." He paused for a long moment. "At least the animals hadn't gotten to him yet."

"If we hadn't come to investigate the site closer, he might not be found for weeks or months. This is pretty isolated."

"Or an animal would have finally taken him."

"Like the wolves." She shivered at the memory of them outside her snow cave, their howls echoing through the night. Fear pricked at her skin like tiny needles.

David leaned over and hoisted Jeremiah up. His body was stiff from the near-zero temperature.

Bree swallowed the lump in her throat and took hold of Jeremiah's feet while David held him by the shoulders.

"At least now the cause of death can be determined," David said between gasps.

Bree didn't reply. It took all her strength to trudge toward the shoreline while carrying Jeremiah's lower half.

When Chance glimpsed them heading toward him, he hurried to Bree and took over for her. "There's no reason to hang around here. I've taken my pictures and assessed what little evidence there was."

"How many people do you think were here?" Bree managed to ask when they reached the bottom of the slope.

"Four, counting the one who must have hidden Jeremiah in the trees." Chance started up the incline.

"The guy went to the stand of evergreens then back. He had to be one strong dude," David said over his shoulder.

"So what were the others doing while he got rid of Jeremiah? I doubt they were out in this weather too long." The cold wind off the lake cut through Bree.

"Setting up the ropes they used to hoist the plane up, I would guess." David ascended the rise a few feet before Chance.

"I'll make some inquiries of the state troopers in this area. I know a couple personally. Maybe someone saw a helicopter flying overhead with a plane dangling below it." Chance panted as he crested the hill. He paused. "I took a week's vacation and flew to Hawaii during Thanksgiving, and I'm paying for it now. Too much good food and not enough exercise."

David laughed. "That was two weeks ago. That's no excuse."

An eerie sound when the wind blew through the surrounding trees made the hairs on Bree's nape stand up. She took David's pole and plowed ahead of the two men. "I'll lead the way." She wanted to get back to Anchorage. This place only held bad memories for her. And fear.

After returning Jeremiah's body to Anchorage the day before, Bree looked forward to going to work at the clinic. She needed to think of something other than her loss. Treating patients could always refocus her on what she loved to do. She stuffed what she needed into her backpack, then slung it over her shoulders and left her house.

Her street still wasn't clear, so she took her alternative mode of transportation. Bree strapped on her skis, then headed for the trail that led into town and the clinic. As she made her way to work, she nodded to several familiar people on the path with her.

At the clinic, she racked her skis and headed to the office she shared with several other part-time volunteer doctors. None of whom were in yet, she noticed. When she entered the room, her attention zeroed in on her desk and her black medical bag. It had been in her missing piece of luggage. How did it get here?

Chilled, she turned in a full circle, checking the office for anyone else. It was empty.

The implication of the bag sitting on her desk renewed the fear she'd felt waiting in her snow cave with the wolves outside.

Bree gasped when one of the nurses poked her head in and said, "You found it. Someone left it here for you early this morning. With your last name engraved on it, I would know your medical bag anywhere."

With her hand over her racing heart, Bree spun toward Gail.

"Sorry, I didn't mean to scare you," the nurse said.

"But I lost the bag." She couldn't take her

eyes off it. "It was my dad's. Using it reminds me of him."

"Good thing someone found it then. Nice to have you back. We have a full schedule today." Gail hugged her, then turned to leave.

"Wait. Did you see anyone drop it off?"

Gail shrugged. "No. It was hanging on the back doorknob when I got here. I was the first person in today. Is there a problem?"

"Yes! The person who stole Jeremiah's plane left it here." Bree inhaled deep breaths, trying to calm herself. Why bring it here? They felt bad about stealing the bag but not the plane? *What is going on*? "I didn't expect it to be here."

Gail came into the room, staring at the black leather bag. "Maybe you should check to make sure everything is there."

For a second the word *bomb* flashed in Bree's mind. She touched Gail's arm and motioned to come with her. They backed away.

Out in the hall, Gail faced Bree. "Do you think something is wrong with the bag?" Her wide blue eyes dominated her expression.

"I don't know. It's mine, but I lost it in dubious circumstances. It shouldn't be here. Remember a couple of years ago when that clinic was bombed across town?"

"Yeah, but that was different. That had to do with drugs."

"We can't take a chance. I'd rather be safe than sorry. We should call the police."

Gail's face paled. "Now you have me scared. What do I do with the patients coming in? The first one should be here in twenty minutes."

"I've got a police detective I can call and ask his advice." Bree had stuck Thomas's card in her purse in her backpack, hoping never to have to use it. But right now she didn't know what was going on and couldn't take any chances. "Get the others out of here while I grab the list of patients. We can call the ones coming this morning from Aurora Café."

While Gail scurried away, Bree snatched up her parka and backpack, digging out the card and her cell phone. As she exited the building with the other doctor, nurse and receptionist, she placed a call to Thomas. She explained what happened with the trip to the wreck site yesterday and the medical bag waiting for her at the clinic. "I'm having everyone leave and go to Aurora Café down the street. Am I overreacting?"

"No, I'm on my way. Inform the businesses on either side of you. I'll meet you at the café. It should be okay there."

Five minutes after following Thomas's direction, she stood at the plate glass window in the café, which gave her a partial view of the clinic. She phoned David. "Now with people evacuating three buildings, I'm feeling foolish," she said after telling him what she had done.

"I'm coming. Is the restaurant far enough away?"

"Yes. Across the street on the next block." She craned her neck to peer down the road. "It looks like the cops are here and closing off traffic."

"I'll come in the back way. See you soon."

Bree hung up and tried to control her rapid heartbeat, but she couldn't seem to drag enough oxygen-rich air into her lungs. Closing her eyes, she sent up a prayer that no one would get hurt.

"Bree, I've taken care of the patients," Gail said as she walked over and leaned against the window and faced her. "You okay?"

"I will be. With the wreck and Jeremiah's death, I'm skating on thin ice." The sounds of the ice cracking the night of the crash echoed in her mind. That was exactly how she'd felt over the past few days. As if the ground beneath her was cracking open. "That bag was lost at the wreck site."

"But isn't it a good thing it was returned to you?"

"The plane has disappeared, and Jeremiah was left outside for the animals to get him."

"Oh," Gail dragged the word out, her eyes growing round again.

She stood next to Bree as they watched the

police clear the area. Thomas arrived at the same time the bomb squad did. While he strode toward the café, a man at the back of the police van suited up in protective gear.

The bell over the door rang as Thomas came into the restaurant. He headed straight for Bree. "The bomb squad will let me know the situation after they've assessed it. All we can do now is watch and wait. On the way here, I talked with David, and he elaborated on what you told me about yesterday. I've asked to be informed of the results of Jeremiah's autopsy. Without the plane, we don't really know what is going on."

Bree gave him a weak smile. "Thanks for coming and not telling me I'm crazy."

"Something is going on involving Jeremiah. I've talked with the drug detail in the department."

Bree straightened, throwing back her shoulders and pivoting toward Thomas.

Before she could say anything, he added, "Just a precaution. I'm not accusing Jeremiah of anything. David said it was a sensitive subject for you."

Bree nodded. "I know you don't have to, but please keep me informed."

"Will do."

David entered through the back door. He greeted them as he approached. The police detective shook his hand, then left, as they noticed the bomb squad officer enter the clinic.

"Nothing yet?" David asked when they were alone.

She shook her head, her throat tight.

David took Bree's arm and tugged her away from the window. "I've had experience with bombs, and I don't want you near glass. Even at a distance it can blow out a window, so let's sit over here." He waved his hand at a corner booth and waited until Bree slid into it before he sat next to her.

Bree scanned the café, noticing the customers had left. The owner remained, as well as the staff of the clinic. "Should I tell them to leave?"

"No, we're okay here or Thomas would have said something."

"Then why are we sitting in this booth?"

"Because I'm a cautious man, and, besides, you don't need to stand there and watch the building. All the action is occurring inside."

"I keep taking you away from your work lately."

"Ella will let me know if I'm needed."

"How about your father? You haven't had a chance to see him much since you rescued me."

"Speaking of my father, I hope you'll come to dinner tonight. If your street doesn't get plowed before that, I'll pick you up on my snowmobile."

Bree drank in the sight of David. As before, his presence made her feel safe. "I hate to intrude on your family time with your father. He's only here for the month."

"He doesn't mind. I called to tell him what was going on at the clinic and that I thought I would have you over for dinner. He's thrilled and already planning what he'll prepare."

"Your father cooks, but you don't?"

David grinned, his eyes glinting. "Some things aren't inherited."

Bree laughed. Lately so much had been serious that laughing felt good. "What can I bring? Dessert? I have some ingredients for a French silk pie."

"If I have to pick you up on the snowmobile, there isn't any place to put it. Although I love chocolate, and I'm open to you fixing me one another time, you don't need to bring anything."

"You've got yourself a deal. It's the least I can do for all you've done for me." She made a mental note to make him the pie as soon as possible.

"Is your daughter coming for Christmas?" she asked him. "I'd love to meet her, too."

The light in David's eyes dimmed. "I think so. At least that's the plan right now."

"You said she is in college. What does she do over the holidays?"

"Work, I guess. Melissa doesn't share her plans with me."

The sadness in his voice touched her. She'd give anything to have both of her parents still alive and in her life. "What happened?"

"Our relationship hasn't been as close as I wish. I used to be gone a lot, and we grew apart. But I hope to change that if she comes this year. I think with Dad here, she'll visit."

"Is she staying long?"

"I'm hoping a week. She liked it here when I was stationed in Alaska."

"How old is she?"

"Nineteen. She took her mother's death hard."

Behind those words there was a wealth of unsaid ones that piqued Bree's curiosity. She really liked David. He'd come into her life when she needed someone. When her fiancé, Anthony, had died only a month before their wedding, she'd learned the hard way not to open herself up to another person.

I can't lose another loved one, Lord, especially like Jeremiah, whom I should have been able to save.

The bell over the door announced someone else entering the café. She pushed the pain back where it belonged—in the past—and leaned forward to look around David. "It's Thomas." She waved her arm, and the detective crossed the restaurant to their booth, sliding in across from her. "Was it a bomb?"

"No. The contents look like what a doctor would have in her medical bag. We examined the items closely, and there was nothing there that could be a bomb."

Thomas leaned forward, his elbows on the table. "Even though there wasn't a bomb in the bag, I'm concerned about how and why it showed up."

David turned to Bree, stabbing her with an intense look. "So am I. It implies a threat. Whoever returned it is telling you he knows you were on the plane and where you are."

"Maybe someone just wanted to return what was mine with no ulterior motive. That medical bag is important to me. For all we know, the plane will show up, too."

A frown carved deep lines into David's face. "You're being naive. You need to treat this as a threat. Right, Thomas?"

The detective dipped his head. "You should be cautious. We don't know why they wanted the plane."

Bree clenched her hands on the table. "But they've got it now. I can't help them. I don't know anything, especially what's really going on. I was only a passenger." She wanted this behind her, so she could focus on something positive.

Thomas rubbed his chin. "Chance did contact the authorities in Daring about the seals. Dead end."

"What if Jeremiah was killed?" David asked.

"We don't know that. When we do, then we'll talk. You two have been used to the darker side of life. You've been trained to look at those possibilities. I haven't. I know Jeremiah wouldn't transport drugs or deal in them. I think someone found any opportunity to salvage a plane. Maybe it's fixable. We don't know." She swung her gaze from David to Thomas. "Is it safe to return to work?"

"Yes, the bomb squad and police are clearing out." Thomas scooted out of the booth. "I'll let the others know they can go back to the clinic."

David remained, blocking her way and angling toward her, a glint of determination in his eyes. "You shouldn't be alone until everything is cleared up."

"And what do you suggest I do?"

"Stay with a relative or friend."

There was no way she would put anyone in danger. She'd dedicated herself to saving lives. "No. I'm fine. I know how to handle a rifle, shotgun and revolver. I have my dad's weapons at the house. My security is good. Besides, I need to decorate for Christmas." Now more than anything she needed to celebrate the meaning of Christ's birth. "I need to get to work. We have patients coming in soon." She signaled for Gail to come over.

Her friend approached the table. "I'll call all the morning patients and try to fit them in today and tomorrow."

David rose. "I'm David Stone."

Gail shook his hand. "Gail Howard. Nice to meet you." She assessed David.

Bree slid from the booth. "I'm going to be working late tonight. Maybe we should postpone the dinner."

"No. The Stone men are flexible. We'll wait for you. When do you think you'll finish?"

"I'll call you after Gail talks with the patients." Bree started for the door with the nurse.

David followed.

At the exit, Bree paused. "You don't need to worry about me, David. I've got tons of people around me at work." She gestured toward the clinic. "And the police are still wrapping everything up. See you later."

As she headed across the four-lane street, she glanced back at the café. David was gone. She'd made it clear she was fine and didn't need him to walk her to the clinic, so why was she disappointed he'd already left?

* * *

"Don, you can cook for me anytime. Your salmon was delicious." Bree took a seat on the couch in the living room at David's house, where a roaring fire made it toasty, cozy.

"I'm glad you liked it. I told my son I was going to eat salmon every other day while in Alaska." David's father took the chair across from her. "He told me about the bomb scare this morning. I've dealt with my share over the years as a police officer."

Bree heard some pans clanging. "Are you sure I can't help David clean up the dinner dishes?"

"Yes. He and I have an agreement. I cook. He cleans up. Besides, you're our guest."

"I understand your granddaughter will be coming in a couple of weeks. Christmas is always so much nicer with family and friends." The second she said it she remembered she wouldn't have that this year. A sense of emptiness—always there since Anthony's and her parents' deaths and now Jeremiah—threatened to overwhelm her.

As Don talked about Melissa coming to Anchorage and what he had planned for them to do, loneliness spread to every part of Bree. She fisted her hands, her fingernails stabbing her palms.

"We used to go all out when my wife was

alive. This year with Melissa coming I wanted to really decorate like we used to. But when I looked for David's decorations, I couldn't find any."

"That's because I don't have any, Dad," David said as he came into the living room, carrying a tray with three mugs on it. "I'm not totally inept in the kitchen, so I made some hot chocolate for everyone."

"With marshmallows?" Bree asked, forcing herself to concentrate on the here and now in the company of two charming men.

David gave her a mug. "Yes, that's the only way to have it. Right, Dad?"

"I taught my son well."

David eased down on the couch, leaving only a foot between Bree and himself. The room's temperature seemed to rise a few degrees. He was easy on the eyes, not to mention he had integrity and compassion for others. It would be so easy to give her feelings free rein, but she knew where that would lead—heartache. She'd already had more than her share.

Bree took a sip of her hot chocolate. "Delicious. So what's this about no Christmas decorations?"

"This is my first Christmas in Alaska. Last year, I celebrated at Dad's." David turned his full attention on his father. "And if I remember correctly, you didn't have any intentions of doing anything until I showed up."

"That's because I thought both you and Melissa weren't going to come to Colorado. Who wants to get everything out for one person?"

Bree cleared her throat. "I do." When both men looked at her, she continued, "I bring the family decorations out because when I put them up I remember how it used to be when my parents were alive. Each ornament on the tree has a story behind it. It's kind of like taking a walk through the past."

David averted his head for a few seconds. When he looked back at her, his expression showed no emotion. "I avoid the past. Let's concentrate on the here and now. If you want decorations, I can get some, Dad. I left all the ones we had before at your house for Melissa. She always loved this time of year."

"She still does. She just spent it with her roommate at college last year." Don watched his son over the rim of his cup as he took a sip.

Something passed between the two men, a tension that seemed to intensify the atmosphere in the living room.

"Then it must be great you two will see her this year," Bree said, trying to lighten the mood.

David pulled his attention away from his father and focused on Bree. "Yes, it will be. So do you want to go shopping with us since it appears you're an expert at decorations?"

Somewhere along the line their conversation had taken on a hidden meaning. She intended to get it back to something more upbeat. "I'd love to accompany you two."

Don threw up his hands, then rose. "I stay away from shopping of any kind. You go without me. I'll be happy with anything. I know it's early, but I'm going to bed. With all that has been going on, I'm exhausted."

"Good night, Don. It was nice to meet you. And thanks for dinner."

David's father nodded and left the room.

Bree glanced at David. "It's eight-thirty. Does he always go to bed this early, or is it something else?"

He exhaled a long breath. "It's me. He and I don't agree with how I handled the situation with my daughter. He missed her at Christmas last year, and I was the reason she didn't come."

"What happened?"

"I wasn't thrilled with who she was dating at the time. She decided to stay with her roommate for the holidays so she could be with her boyfriend." He rubbed his hand along his jaw. "Not two months later, they broke up. He was dating other girls behind her back."

"Then she must realize the wisdom in what

you saw about the guy. Has she said anything to you about it?"

"No, we haven't talked in a year. She doesn't return my calls or texts."

"And she's coming here for Christmas? Are you sure?"

"No, but Dad insists he got her to promise. Frankly, I won't believe it until I see her."

She wanted to ask what went wrong with their relationship, but that conversation implied a deeper bond between them, which she wanted to avoid. "I hope she does. For you and your dad." She finished the last of her hot chocolate. "I better leave. I have a full day tomorrow at the clinic. Some of the morning patients were crammed into an already busy day."

"I know what you mean. There is some maintenance I need to do on the plane." He picked up the tray with the empty cups and headed toward the kitchen.

Bree trailed after him, wishing now that she had driven to his house. But he'd insisted on picking her up. Like a date? No, just two new friends sharing some time together, getting to know each other.

She slipped on her coat, gloves and hat while he did likewise; then he opened the door to the garage. "I enjoyed tonight."

As she passed him, he clasped her hand and

stilled her. "So did I. Dad is full of great stories. I liked hearing him tell them again."

"He is quite entertaining."

"I can tell he likes you." David moved into the garage and shut the kitchen door.

"How?"

"When he doesn't care for someone, he doesn't say more than a few words. He hardly gave us time to talk during dinner."

Bree chuckled, thinking back to the pleasant meal. It reminded her of the times she'd spent with Jeremiah. "Do you think he'll move to Anchorage?"

"I hope he does. He loves the outdoors. Alaska will be perfect for him."

"And it's nice to have family closer."

David opened the passenger door for Bree. "Yes, it is." When she was inside, he made his way around the hood of the car and slid behind the steering wheel, then punched the remote for the garage door. "As a kid we went hiking, fishing, hunting and camping all the time. Mom, Dad and me. I was an only child."

"Me, too, and my family did the same. Although I've lived here most of my life, I still haven't done and seen all I want of Alaska."

"I missed doing that with my own family."

"Because of being in the service?"

David backed out of his driveway and headed

toward her house. "No, the main reason was my wife didn't like any of those things. Melissa and I did a little depending on where I was stationed, but not as much as I would have liked."

"I hope I get a chance to meet her." *Why did I say that*? Because she wanted to know everything she could about David. But he kept a lot of himself locked away. She wasn't sure she would ever really know him, which was probably a good thing. The more she discovered about him, the more she liked him.

At an intersection, he stopped to wait his turn and smiled at her. "I hope you'll get to meet Melissa, too."

Her pulse rate kicked up a notch. In the shadows, she could feel the intensity behind his look and the genuineness in his grin. Even with the temperature hovering around zero and the heater not having a chance to warm the interior yet, his look had done the job.

When he turned onto her street, she almost wished the evening were longer, but she hadn't slept well since the wreck. Weariness wheedled its way through her. She needed a good night of rest, without the nightmares.

He pulled into her driveway and switched off the engine. "I'll give you a call about a time to go shopping for the decorations tomorrow."

"Good. You have my cell number. I always

carry it." She grasped the handle and pushed it down. "Thanks. Tell your dad again how much I loved the dinner."

As she exited the car, David did, too. "I'm walking you to your door."

"You don't have to. This isn't a date." Then why did it feel like it was? Wishful thinking?

"Humor me." He started for the sidewalk leading to her porch, pausing until she caught up, then strolling next to her.

She unlocked her door, then swung toward him. "Good night."

"I'd like to check and make sure your house is secure. Okay?"

"I overreacted this morning. I'm not in danger." *At least I don't think so.* "I'm fine."

"Please. Checking will give me peace of mind so I get some sleep tonight."

She shoved open her door and hurried to tap in the security code on the panel in the hallway off the foyer. When the beeping stopped, she returned. "See, perfectly all right. My security system is working well, and don't forget my guns."

"If anything happened to you…" David's voice faded into silence as he headed for the kitchen and checked the back door and the one to the garage. Then he went from room to room, making sure the windows were locked.

In the living room, Ringo saw him and came over to rub against him and whine. David bent over and scratched the big white cat behind the ears.

Bree leaned against the doorjamb. "He doesn't do that usually. It takes a while for him to warm up to a stranger like that."

"I like animals. I've thought of getting one now that I have regular hours. Strike that. Not exactly regular but a cat's pretty independent and can be left a couple of days by himself. Are you going to keep him?"

"In January I'll be going to a village and will be gone for a month, so I was going to look for someone to keep him, at least while I was away."

David straightened. "Then you don't have to look anymore. I'll take care of him when you are away."

"Thanks. At least I won't have to worry about Ringo."

David moved toward her. "Good." He took her hands and edged closer. "Your house is locked up tight. I know you told me that, but I'm one of those guys who has to see it for himself. I appreciate you humoring me."

Jeremiah used to watch out for her, and she'd let him although she'd always felt she could take care of herself. She didn't know if she wanted

David to feel he had to take on that role. It took their friendship to another level—one she wasn't ready to pursue.

She should step back, but the soft look in his eyes captured her and held her rooted to the spot, mere inches from him. When she drew in a breath, she inhaled his scent, it was like the forest they'd walked through the day before.

He lifted his hand to cup her jawline, the warm imprint searing his brand into her. At least that was the feeling that overcame her as he framed her face and slowly dipped his head toward hers.

SIX

Ever since David had found Bree safe and secure at the café, he'd wanted to hold her, kiss her, protect her. He brushed his lips across hers. She wound her arms around him, anchoring her against him. Her vanilla scent surrounded him as he deepened the kiss.

When she drew back, her dazed look no doubt mirrored his. He hadn't kissed a woman since his wife. The thought of their last one, the morning he had left for his final tour of duty in the Middle East, sobered him. He had no business starting something with Bree when he didn't have his past in order.

He shut down his emotions and put more space between them. "I'd better go. I'm going to the airport early in the morning." He crossed the foyer. When she didn't say anything, he glanced over his shoulder.

He wanted to kiss her again. Until his sanity edged the insanity of that action out of the way.

"Good night," he murmured and escaped from the house.

He didn't leave the porch, though, until he heard her lock the door. Then he practically raced away before he made a fool of himself. He hadn't gone inside with the intention of kissing her. He'd only wanted to assure himself she was safe—a purely selfish reason so he could sleep tonight without worrying.

Worrying is a waste of time. His father's words came unbidden into David's mind. One part of him knew God was in control and he should let Him do what He did best. But he was a man of action and couldn't give that last bit of control over to God.

In the living room Bree watched David back out of her driveway and head down the cleared street. The lamp near the curb gave off a golden glow that lit a small area of her yard, but most of it was in shadows and darkness. She switched off the overhead light, went back to the large window and peeked out at the night.

Not one evergreen moved. The wind was still, in stark contrast to a couple of days ago when it had snowed with almost blizzard-like conditions. In a short time her life had changed. She'd lost Jeremiah, her last link to her parents. She'd gotten to know David and realized the danger in getting too close. She needed to cut their ties before she lost her heart to him and he broke it.

She'd seen the look he'd given her after their kiss. It had been full of confusion and something she couldn't quite decipher. Regret? Maybe.

A movement outside caught her attention. She squinted her eyes and tried to focus better on a spot near a fir tree. Was someone out there?

Her thundering heartbeat pulsated inside her head, drowning out all thoughts for a few seconds.

Then one flooded her mind. *Get your gun.*

She swirled from the window and hurried upstairs to her bedside table. She pulled open the drawer where she kept the loaded revolver. It was gone!

Her rapid breathing sounded in the eerie silence of her house. She closed her eyes to the spinning room and collapsed on her bed.

Think. No sign of a break-in. Is this where I put it after cleaning it before leaving for Daring?

When she tried to retrace her steps that day before she'd left, all she could think about was the emergency she'd been called back to the clinic to help with. She fumbled in her pocket and withdrew her cell phone. She should call David and tell him she couldn't find her revolver.

What if someone had gotten into her house and taken it?

She jumped to her feet and covered the distance to her walk-in closet to search for the rifle and shotgun she stored there. Both hung on the back wall above her rack of shoes. She took the shotgun, loaded it and returned to the bedroom. Cell phone in one hand and her weapon in the other, she began checking the few places she kept her revolver if not in the bedside table.

All of them were empty.

She went back to the living room window and peered out between the slats. That same pitch-black patch drew her attention. Short of going outside and investigating, she couldn't tell if someone was standing there or not.

Ringo brushed against her legs, sending a streak of alarm through her until his loud cry for food penetrated that fear. She went into the kitchen to get his chow and paused at the table where she'd cleaned her gun the last time.

She remembered that Jeremiah had sat across from her, keeping her entertained with stories from one of his trips up north. Her cell phone had rung. She'd hurried to get her keys and drive to the clinic. The last thing she'd done as she'd left the house was ask Jeremiah to finish cleaning her gun and put her weapon in the drawer by the front door.

She found her revolver and sank against the hall table. Now she remembered why it was there. He'd told her when she'd left that she needed it near where she would come into the house.

Stuffing her cell phone back into her pocket, she propped her shotgun against the wall near the front door, then took up guard at the window to see if anyone was outside. Too much trauma had occurred the past few days. It wasn't like her to forget something like that. What if there had been a problem? She knew what stress could do to a person. She needed a good night's sleep, and after being posted at the window for half an hour and not seeing anyone or any movement, she decided she'd overreacted.

She checked the alarm and the doors, then went to her bedroom, leaving the revolver on her bedside table next to her charging cell phone. In time everything would return to normal and the wreck would become a distant memory—she hoped.

Late the next afternoon after a long day at the clinic, Bree stood next to a cart in a large department store. "You don't have to buy out the whole Christmas section. Save some for other customers."

David dropped the set of glitter-covered ornaments

into the basket. "I'm not like you. I'm starting from scratch. I need it all. Lights. Ornaments. Tinsel."

"Are you an all-or-nothing kind of guy?"

He nodded and snatched up several boxes of lights. "Dad reminded me how much Melissa loved Christmas. Maybe if I can re-create some of that—" He stopped, stared at the pile already in the cart, then looked at Bree.

Astonished and appalled expressions vied for dominance on his face.

"I think you have enough lights to light up the whole street," Bree said in a soft voice.

"It won't work, will it?"

She thought she knew what he meant, but she asked anyway. "What won't work?"

"Trying to relive the past. This won't bring back my daughter and make a bad relationship good."

"The only thing that can do that is you and Melissa working things out. Possessions don't make a difference. People do."

"I first have to get her here and make her agree to talk to me. These past few years have been so hard, trying to make amends for regrets but at the same time letting her know my side of what happened."

"Make it simple." Bree smiled, thinking of her boxes of decorations. There was nothing simple about them, but they were an accumulation of years of memories. "Instead of grabbing all these ornaments, think about what you like. What Melissa likes. Your dad. An ornament can reflect that. For instance, when my parents found out that I wanted to be a doctor, they started buying ones that had a medical theme. My dad got particular pleasure in buying them since he was a doctor. What does your daughter like to do? What's her major?"

"She likes to ski. She has changed her major twice, but right now she wants to teach elementary school. She also loves to watch sports and played soccer all the way through school. And she loves to read."

"All those can give you good choices for ornaments for the tree. I know a store we can go to for those."

David started restocking the shelves with boxes from his cart, except for the lights and garland. "Let's go."

Twenty minutes later he positioned himself in front of a wall of unique wooden and hand-painted ornaments. While he studied them and picked several, Bree locked onto a biplane that would have been perfect for Jeremiah. She took if off the shelf when David was looking away. She couldn't give it to Jeremiah, but she could give it to David. She went to the checkout and paid for it, then stuck it in her purse.

When she found David again, he was in another part of the store. The small basket he carried was nearly full. The look on his face reminded her of the first time she'd come in to browse the beautifully handmade items.

"Look at this. Chess pieces as ornaments." David pointed to another area in the Christmas shop. "Dad would love this. Melissa, too. He taught her to play. She was getting good. Even beat him once or twice."

"Do you play?"

"No, how about you?"

She shook her head. "I like to do jigsaw puzzles. Every time I go to a village, I take one or two to work on in the evening."

"My dad does those, especially in the winter."

"Do you?"

"No."

"You mentioned you like carpentry before. Does that take up all your free time?"

"I also like activities outdoors, but I often carve. Sometimes I make a piece of furniture. I have a woodshop out back at my house. I've sold a couple of tables and chairs. Now I'm working on making a coffee table for my living room."

"I can't picture you as a carpenter."

"What do you picture me as?"

"An outdoorsman."

David started for the cashier at the front of the store. "I am. That's one of the reasons I came to Alaska. There's so much to see and do here."

"And having a plane allows you to do that."

"There are some places that having a plane makes it much easier to get to." David blocked her view of the decorations he passed to the cashier to ring up.

After giving the woman behind the counter his credit card, he grabbed the paper bag and headed toward the door. "I'm actually eager to get the tree up and see what you think of my selection of ornaments."

"What were they besides the chess pieces?"

He winked at her as he opened the passenger door. "You'll just have to wait and see."

"Did you get me one?"

He nodded and backed out of the parking space. "I have a special one for you that I want you to put on my tree. I know you don't have any family here, so I'm adopting you into mine this Christmas. I don't want you to be alone this holiday."

A knot swelled into her throat from the sweet gesture. She had to swallow several times before she thought her voice wouldn't crack when she said, "Gail and her husband, John, a lieutenant in the air force have invited me to their house for Christmas day. She's the nurse I work with at the clinic. You met her at the café. We're good friends."

"Speaking of the clinic, do you ski to work every day while there's snow?"

"No, but several times a week, weather permitting. It's my exercise. Otherwise I just sit around and eat bonbons and drink hot chocolate."

"Please do me a favor."

"What?"

"Drive to work or let me take you. You'll be safer if you're not out in the open on a trail."

The earnest look on his face urged her to agree. "I won't ski to work anymore."

"Thanks." A brilliant smile transformed his worried expression. "So eating bonbons and drinking hot chocolate appeals to you, too. Are you a chocoholic like me?"

"Well, maybe just a tiny bit."

His gaze sliced to her as he turned onto his street. "I hope you'll choose to do both. Go to Gail's house and then come to mine."

"But it will be a family Christmas for you, Melissa and your dad."

"I may need backup with Melissa," he said, pulling into his driveway.

"I'm not sure my presence would be the best

for you. Melissa might misread our relationship. You said she took her mother's death hard."

After switching off the engine, David shifted toward her. "What is our relationship?"

"Friends, of course," she said quickly, as though stating it made it true. Frankly, she couldn't shake the feeling it was much more, which was frightening.

"Yes, friends." He turned and opened his door. "Dad has fixed some soup and sandwiches for us while we decorate the tree."

If she kept seeing David every day and spending the evenings with him, her heart was going to be broken. There was part of himself he kept hidden. Even if she had wanted a relationship beyond friendship, she needed all of a person. She wanted a marriage like her parents'. Their closeness and love for each other had been infectious. Guilt gnawed at her, never giving her the peace she wanted. She'd thought she would have it with Anthony, but he'd died six years ago and taken her dreams with him. If only she hadn't dared him to race her down that mountain...

"Are you two sure you don't want to wait until Melissa arrives?" Bree asked as she watched the two men wrestle with putting the artificial tree together.

"She never wanted to help with putting the decorations up, but she always enjoyed them. Besides, she won't be here until two days before Christmas." Don tossed a fake branch over his shoulder and pulled out another, trying it in the hole.

"Dad, that isn't right."

Bree scooped up the directions to the tree and waved them in the air. "If you two would stop and read these, you'll have it together in no time."

David glanced up. "What?"

"Directions. They fell out when you grabbed all the pieces."

"When we finish with this, I think you should keep it up year-round. A cut real tree is so much easier." Don took the paper from Bree and studied it.

"Until the needles fall off, usually all at once. I've got the perfect closet for this thing." David looked over his father's shoulder at the directions. "I didn't see these numbers."

Bree retrieved a branch near her and pointed to the end of it. "Right here."

"Oh. That should make it a little easier." David took it from her and immediately found the slot it fit in.

Bree shook her head and backed away while the two men hurriedly stuck branches in the center pole. "I'm glad the lights are new and not left over from last year. I can't imagine what you guys would do with a bundle of knotted lights."

Don snorted. "I'd never do that. I have a system."

David roared with laughter. "I remember that one year you threw a snared mess away and went out and bought new lights."

Don glared at his son. "I learn from my mistakes. Where do you think my system came from?"

Bree leaned against the back of the couch, relishing the moment with David and his father. For a brief while she felt like a member of a family. She longed for that, but the risk was just too high for her.

Fifteen minutes later, David swept his arm toward the fake tree. "There. Put together with lights on it. I told you we'd get it done."

Bree checked her watch. "But it's time for me to go home now. I have work tomorrow."

David swiveled toward the clock on the mantel. "It's only seven. We've got time, and you can still be home at a reasonable hour. Besides, you haven't seen all my ornaments or the one I got with you in mind."

Don pushed himself to his feet. "You two work on that. I'll fix the hot chocolate tonight. David told me you were a chocoholic. Welcome to my club. Love the stuff. So does my son. That he did inherit from me."

As she helped David put the pieces of a chess set on the tree, he yawned. "Are you sure about me staying? That's the third time tonight you've done that."

One corner of his mouth quirked up, a dimple appearing in his cheek. "I didn't sleep well last night."

"Why?" she asked. As for herself, she'd finally gotten the rest she'd needed.

"I worried about you. I don't think you should be alone. Just in case."

"In case what?"

"What if someone is after you? We can't ignore the white helicopter."

"Pirates."

David finished hanging a rook and faced her. "We don't know that's what's going on."

"Why else did they take the plane unless they wanted it? Maybe they assessed they could repair it. The front end didn't go into the water. At least I don't think so, or they would have had a hard time getting it out."

But David was unconvinced. "You could stay here, or I could stay at your place until the police figure out what happened to Jeremiah."

"No. I think he had a heart attack, and I don't want to make this into more than it is. Besides, my gun is right beside my bed." She remembered the momentary panic the night before but didn't tell David about that. He'd worry even more and insist she not be alone. She'd been living on her own for several years and was doing fine. Nor did she want to interrupt his time with his family any more than she already had. "If we find out Jeremiah was murdered, then I will consider it. Okay?"

"A deal." He shook her hand. "I'm going to give Chance a call and see if he can hurry the autopsy along."

With a heavy sigh, Bree looked toward the ceiling. "Do something, God."

He pulled out his cell phone. "I'm sorry I'm being a pain, but I didn't rescue you to have something bad happen." He began punching in numbers.

"What do you think? You're responsible for me? You aren't and—"

David waved her quiet. "Hi, Chance. This is David. I'm checking to see what you've heard about Jeremiah's autopsy. Call me. I'll be up—" he pointedly looked at Bree "—late tonight."

Bree pressed her lips together and tried not to laugh. She couldn't contain it. "You don't play fair."

"I play to win." His smile dazzled her.

"I thought you two would have the tree decorated by now. I waited as long as I could," Don said as he came in carrying three mugs. He gave one to both of them.

For the next hour, they drank hot chocolate and decorated the tree. Then Bree remembered she had the ornament for David in her purse. She went to retrieve it from the hall table and when she returned, she was struck by the white lights blazing as though the tree were on fire.

"I think you have enough lights." Bree handed the tissue-wrapped plane to David while she gave Don an ornament of a moose to symbolize Alaska. "I hope when you put this on your tree in the next years," she told Don, "you remember me."

Don smiled warmly. "I won't forget you."

David remained quiet, staring at his gift. When his gaze locked with hers, he murmured, "I love this. I used to have a model of this kind of plane when I was a kid."

"Good. Now put them on the tree, and it will be complete."

"Not quite. I wanted an ornament that would remind me of you, so I got you this." David bent over and pulled something from the paper bag.

Bree opened the box to reveal a small stethoscope. "I love it."

"I bought two stethoscopes. One for this tree

and one for yours. I tried to find a medical bag, but the store didn't have one."

"I haven't got one like this. It'll fit in with my other medical ornaments. Thanks. And I haven't forgotten you owe me a duffel bag," she teased him.

"I intend to go back when the snow thaws in the spring and check thoroughly."

"I told Melissa I would send her a picture." Don moved back and snapped the photo with his cell phone. "I think she's looking forward to a break. This last semester she had some tough classes."

Bree peered at David, whose jaw was set in a hard line. She could easily read his mind. He was upset that his father knew more about his daughter than he did.

But David recovered quickly and took out his own phone. "I think I'll take a picture to show Ella I really did get a tree. My assistant won't believe that I agreed to have one. She tried to get me to buy one right after Thanksgiving."

As David took the photo, his cell phone rang. The sound surprised him, and he dropped the phone but recovered it before it hit the floor. He answered quickly. "What did you find out?" His forehead creased. "Really? Are you sure?"

A long pause. He finished the call with, "She's right here. I'll tell her."

Bree grew tense. It had to be Chance with the results of Jeremiah's autopsy.

SEVEN

"Was that Chance?" Bree asked David the second he disconnected the call.

He nodded. "There was no indication that Jeremiah was poisoned or that his death wasn't anything but a heart attack."

"So he died from natural causes," his dad said. As Don contemplated the news, he rubbed his chin, a habit he had when he wasn't sure about something.

"What aren't you saying, Dad?"

"Just a hunch. I don't think whatever is going on is over."

"What's going on?" There was a frantic tone to Bree's question.

His father shrugged. "Probably nothing." He waved his hand in the air then pivoted and headed for the hallway. "Ignore this old cop who looks for the worst in everything."

When he left the room, Bree asked, "What do you think?"

"At this point you may be right. Pirates salvaging the plane." He shook his head. "I don't know if the plane could have been salvaged, though. I didn't get a good look at all the damage. My single thought was getting you out of there. But we can't dismiss the fact that someone broke into Jeremiah's house, looking for something. What was on his tablet? Is anything else missing?"

"We may never know that. I'm sure I don't know everything he had, and I haven't even had the time to go back there to search further. Maybe tomorrow." She averted her gaze, staring off to the side of David. "I need to go through his possessions but..."

He took two steps and crowded into Bree's personal space. The pain behind her last words wrenched him. "I'll help you. You don't have to do it alone. Unless an emergency comes up, I can work tomorrow with you on Jeremiah's house." He reached out and took her hands in his to still their trembling. "Chance is still looking into the helicopter I described to him. Something might come up to shed light on what's going on."

"I know I've said this before, but I hate to take you away from your dad. He's only here for the month."

"Don't worry. He'll be the first to suggest I help you."

She expelled a loud breath. "Thanks. I haven't been able to go back inside his house. I've been using the excuse of work to avoid what I need to do. I know I have to meet with the lawyer soon about Jeremiah's will and give him an account of what Jeremiah has in the house..." Her brows knitted. "But are you sure? Jeremiah's house can wait if—"

David pressed a finger to her lips. "Shh. If it will make you feel better, I'll bring Dad along. This is right up his alley. And he might have insight into what happened. He's the cop in the family, not me."

"Only if he wants—"

He stopped her doubts by kissing her, pulling her against him and winding his arms around her. When they parted, he touched his forehead to hers. "For the twenty years before I retired, my life was directed by others. I spent a good part of that career in combat situations. Now I can do what I want, and I want to help you. I have chosen to oversee Northern Frontier Search and Rescue because I get a lot out of helping others—the kind of help I want to do. Okay? Do we have a date to clean Jeremiah's tomorrow afternoon?"

Her eyes shone, and she gave him a nod. The

appeal in her look enticed him to kiss her again, but he held back. She needed a friend now more than anything, and he wasn't sure he was good at anything more than that.

The next afternoon Bree stood in the middle of the chaos in Jeremiah's living room while David walked with Don through the small house. She didn't know if she could do this. The disarray before her seemed like frenzy driven with a touch of panic and rage. The room mirrored her emotions—disorderedly and in disrepair.

When she was a child, her mother used to read her nursery rhymes, and she'd always felt sorry for Humpty Dumpty who fell off the wall and shattered into pieces. That was where she was at the moment. On top of the wall, teetering.

Lord, what's going on? Why has this happened? Why did You take Jeremiah, too?

David and his dad entered the living room as Don noted, "This is going to take a while."

Shutting the door on the feelings nipping at her composure, she swung around and plastered a neutral expression on her face. "That's an understatement. Any suggestions on how to go about doing this? David and I did a little the other day, but as you can see, it didn't make much of a dent in the mess."

"One room at a time," David replied. "Maybe target in here first since it's what you see when you come into the house. Then when we come back, we'll see the accomplishment. How does that sound?" He removed his heavy overcoat, righted a chair and laid it on the seat.

When David said *we*, she relished that word. She liked knowing she wasn't alone in this. "Sounds like a good plan." Bree took off her parka and set it on top of David's. "I'll take the desk drawers and their contents on the floor."

"I'll put the books in the bookcases." Don moved toward the wall lined with shelves, stepping around the piles underfoot.

"And I'll straighten up and right the furniture." David picked up a chair.

As Bree worked on the desk, she investigated any crevice or cubbyhole she found. Her actions became automatic while she blanked her mind. But every once in a while, an object would spark a memory. When she found a photo of her and Jeremiah posing by his plane in Daring during the summer, tears jammed her throat. Only five months ago. She remembered the flight back to Anchorage. Jeremiah had taken a detour as he often did to show her some bears in a rushing stream, catching their dinner. A tear splashed on her hand, pulling her out of the memory. She couldn't cry again. It wouldn't change what happened. A headache began to form behind her eyes.

A hand clasped her shoulder, and she looked back at David leaning over her. She tried to re-assure him with a smile, but she couldn't.

"Okay?"

"Just thinking about the past. I keep running into things that remind me of something Jeremiah did with my family or me. I didn't real-ize he was such a pack rat." She held up a ticket stub. "This is to a movie he took Mom and me to see. It was one of those weepy romances, and his snores filled the theater. Mom had a hard time waking him up. We were getting some nasty stares the whole time."

David laughed. "I can see Jeremiah doing that."

"Bree, did you say his tablet was stolen?" Don asked from the other end of the living room.

Taking David's hand, Bree rose. "Yes. Why?"

"Is this it?"

She nodded. "Where was it?"

"Buried under the books on the floor. The screen is cracked. Maybe that's why it was left behind, but in that case, why did they leave be-hind this coin collection?"

"What coin collection?" Bree strode to where Don stood in front of a cabinet.

"Right there in a black box."

David joined her and stooped to retrieve the container, then open the lid. He whistled. "How did they miss it? There are a couple of gold coins as well as some very old ones. This may be valuable."

"I didn't know about the coins. Not that I had to be informed, but I always thought he told me everything. He was always grumbling about not having enough money, so how did he buy these, especially the gold ones?" Confusion reigned as she stared at the large box, full to the top. "Maybe the lawyer will know something about this when I have my meeting with him in a few days." She scanned the room. "What else do I not know about? Was there something else that was valuable that the robbers actually took?"

The pounding in her head increased, and all she wanted to do was go to bed and pull the covers over her head. She thought she'd known Jeremiah well.

Don flipped his hand toward the box. "This makes me think they were after something specific and the other stuff wasn't worth their time."

"What?" Bree asked, massaging her temples.

"I don't know. It could be a lot of things. The first thing that comes to mind is drugs."

She couldn't buy that. Jeremiah had an aversion to illegal drugs. He didn't understand giving up that kind of control for a momentary "feel good."

Bree shook her head violently and backed away from the pair as though that would erase the possibility. "No. That I'm sure of." *But am I*?

She stumbled on something behind her and started to go down. David lunged for her and caught her, his outdoorsy scent flooding her senses. He'd been there for her from the beginning. For a few seconds all she wanted to do was stay in his arms and feel the safety of his embrace.

"Okay?" David murmured close to her ear.

She nodded and stepped away before she became too accustomed to his support. "So it's very possible whatever they were looking for, they got, and I might never know what it was."

"Right," Don said. "The coins were poured out all over this cabinet, so whoever broke in went through the box. I guess it's possible there was one or more they were specifically looking for."

David came around from behind Bree and faced her. "My suggestion is to finish in here and take a break. It doesn't all have to be done in a day."

She panned the partially restored living room, comforted for that at least. "I agree."

"And I'm calling Thomas to let him know we found the tablet. He may want to take a look at it, but without any more evidence, there'll be little he can do, especially since it seems that Jeremiah died from a heart attack, not foul play."

As Bree went back to work on the drawer contents, she tried to feel comforted that the burglars probably found what they were looking for and life would go back to normal. At least she prayed that was the case.

"Did you enjoy your day off?" Gail asked Bree a couple of days later at the clinic.

Bree finished her note in the patient's chart, then closed it and turned toward her friend. "If cleaning Jeremiah's house is considered fun, then yes."

"Duty calls. I know what that's like. I also know how much you love housework."

"I hear a note of sarcasm in your voice."

Gail smiled and held up two fingers an inch apart. "Just a little bit."

"At least Jeremiah's house looks almost normal again, especially thanks to David and his dad."

"That's great. Anyone who will help you clean up a trashed house is a keeper. If I hadn't been scheduled to work, I could have helped you, but I imagine you had more fun with him," Gail said with a laugh.

"I have to admit David is easy on the eyes, but in no way was cleaning up fun." Bree noticed Gail was dressed in her heavy overcoat, snow boots, hat and gloves. "Going somewhere?"

"Yes, I have to pick up John from the base, but when I went to leave, I found my car dead. The battery again. I need to own stock in a battery company. The cold is murder on them. I thought I would bring John back with one, and he can change it out. Husbands are good for a couple of things."

"I wouldn't know, but you do have a special man. You can use my car. I'm not going anywhere." Bree came around the counter and walked back to her office. When she'd retrieved her keys, she dropped them in Gail's hand.

"I saw how David looked at you in the café the other day," the nurse said. "You could have a special man, too."

The heat of a blush singed her cheeks. "With all that I'm dealing with, I'm not looking."

"You should be. You're thirty. Practically an old maid."

Laughter welled up in Bree, and its release

eased the tension of the past few days. "You've only been married two years and you're thirty-four."

"Exactly. I'm speaking from experience." Gail curled her gloved hands around the keys and swung around. "Thanks. I'll be back in about an hour. Do you want me to bring you anything for lunch?"

"Nope. I'm meeting David for lunch at the café in twenty minutes."

"A date! That's great."

"Not a date…" Suddenly she realized she wished it was. "Chance, a friend of David's who is a state trooper, wants to talk with us about Jeremiah's missing plane."

Gail paused at the door and said, "Maybe you can mix pleasure with business." Then she winked and left.

No, she couldn't—not the kind of pleasure Gail was referring to. David and she could only be friends. Everything was happening too fast. She needed to slow things down.

Bree glanced at her watch and decided to update a couple more charts before she left. Then she grabbed her coat and purse, and entered Aurora Café right on time. She found David and Chance at a table in the back.

As she made her way to them, she zeroed in on David's face. His scowl indicated that he didn't like what Chance was saying. Both men were so intent on their conversation that they didn't realize she was in the café until she stopped next to David.

When his gaze latched on to hers, his expression morphed into a neutral one as he stood and pulled out a chair next to him. "You're early."

"No, I'm on time. How long have you two been here?"

"Five or ten minutes," David said with a shrug.

After taking a seat, Bree homed in on Chance on her left. "Okay, tell me what you told him and don't sugarcoat anything. I already know it's something I don't want to hear."

Chance looked at David, who nodded, then retuned his gaze to her. "We think we've found the remains of what's left of Jeremiah's plane."

"That's good." Her stiff shoulders sagged.

"It's going to be hard to climb down to check it at least until late spring, but the type and color are the same. Can't read any markings on it. It's smashed and scattered all over a deep creviced ravine in the Alaska Range."

"Which probably means it wasn't pirates looking to salvage a plane." David's clipped words echoed the strain on his face.

"Also there was one sighting of the helicopter with the plane. A man heard a chopper and looked out as it went over his cabin. Heading southwest, which fits with where the remains of the plane were found."

"Maybe the line holding the aircraft snapped." Bree needed to believe it was someone trying to salvage a wreck.

Chance pinched his lips together. "It's a possibility, but I'm more inclined to think someone wanted the plane for other reasons. Like drugs. Or something on the black market."

Bree opened her mouth to deny it again but instead swallowed her protest. After going through Jeremiah's house and putting it back in order as best she could, she couldn't vehemently deny his involvement in anything. Even though Jeremiah had always talked about the dangers of drinking, she'd found several empty bottles of alcohol at the bottom of one pile and a full bottle in a kitchen cabinet.

Chance rose. "I wish I could stay and join you for lunch. But I'm headed to work. I'll let you know if I hear anything else." He peered at her. "Please be careful. If they haven't found what they're looking for, no telling what they'll do."

Bree shivered and folded her arms over her chest. The last couple of nights after the wreck she'd come to believe there wasn't anyone observing her house. They would have made their move by now. It was too cold to stand outside and watch her like that, her practical side pointed out.

But also she'd been lured into a sense of safety with the feeling that the robbers got what they came for. And there was an off chance that the break-in had nothing to do with the people in the helicopter. Add to that, now she didn't know what to think about Jeremiah and what he might have been involved with.

After the waitress took their orders, a silence hovered between her and David as though neither one wanted to talk because that meant they needed to discuss what Chance had told them.

Finally when the waitress brought them their coffee, Bree said, "Do you think it's Jeremiah's plane?"

"Yes, most likely. From what Chance said to me before you came, the pilot who spotted it flies over that area several times a week, and he hasn't seen anything there before yesterday. He flew as low as he could and checked it out, looking for bodies. There were none he could find. There wasn't a distress call or emergency locator signal, either."

"Anything else on the white helicopter?" She fiddled with her spoon, restless energy vying with her weariness.

"No." He sipped his coffee. When he set it down, he angled toward her, covering her hand with his on the table. "I think the worst part of all of this is we don't know what's going on. We should err on the side of caution. Please reconsider coming to stay at my house until we know more. I spoke to Dad last night, and he hoped you would accept my invitation. He's enjoyed your visits, but more important, he's concerned for your safety."

Bree listened to David, almost as if she were a spectator to the conversation. She wanted to deny the danger. The closest she had ever come to being in danger before the wreck was when a patient went berserk in the ER because he needed drugs, but security was always there quickly.

"Bree?"

She blinked, realizing that David was waiting for her to say something. She took a breath and looked at him. "I like your dad. He reminds me of mine, except for his occupation. My father is one of the reasons I went into medicine." And she wished he were there right now. *Thankfully I still have You, Lord, because I don't know what to do about all of this.*

"What are you going to do when your daughter comes in nine days?"

"Talk to her about the situation."

"It's one thing if I'm there with you and your dad. Both of you are very capable of taking care of yourself. But what if my presence puts your daughter's life in danger?"

"We have nine days before we have to make a decision about that."

"Let me think about it. I can call you later before I go home from the clinic."

"You've been driving to work, haven't you?"

"Yes, worrywart. I'm going to blame you when I put on a few pounds because I'm not exercising like I should. Well, that and your dad's cooking."

"I can compromise. We can go skiing on some trails by my house."

"Good. I'm an outdoor kind of gal, even in the winter. That's one of the things I love about Alaska."

"Me, too." He squeezed her hand, then released it while the waitress served them their hamburgers and sweet potato fries.

After the waitress topped off their coffees, Bree bowed her head and said, "Father, please give us wisdom in dealing with what's going on. Bless this food and David and his dad for their kind offer."

"My offer is what's best for me. I wouldn't get any sleep if I knew you were in danger. In fact, I haven't. I'm a desperate man. I need my rest." A smile danced in his eyes.

She loved seeing it after the heavy conversation they'd been having. Maybe she would sleep better at David's house instead of listening for any unusual sounds. She started to tell him yes when his cell phone beeped. He read his text, the smile vanishing.

"I've got to go to work."

"What's wrong?"

"A child has gone missing in a small town north of here. I'll be part of an aerial search while it's still daylight."

"That's only a few hours."

"I know. But there are ground teams going out, too." He removed his wallet.

"I'll take care of the bill. Take your hamburger with you. It might be a long day."

"Thanks." He snatched his hamburger off the plate and strode toward the exit.

When he left, the energy seemed to be siphoned from the café. Suddenly she didn't want to sit by herself and finish her lunch. She wrapped up her food, paid for it and hurried toward the clinic. She could eat in the break room. Maybe Gail was back, and she could ask her opinion of staying at David's.

But the room was empty, so she went to her office, worked on some files stacked on her desk and ate her hamburger. When the receptionist paused in the doorway, Bree looked up.

"Has the first afternoon patient arrived?" Bree asked, pushing her chair back and standing.

"Not yet. I just got a call from Gail's husband. She hasn't arrived to pick him up. Didn't she leave over an hour ago?"

Glancing at her watch, Bree frowned. "An hour and a half ago. Have you tried her cell phone?"

The receptionist nodded. "Goes to voice mail."

Bree checked her cell phone for messages in case Gail had an accident or Bree's car had broken down. Nothing. "I'll call John back. It's probably nothing. She was running a couple of errands. Maybe they took longer than she thought. Let me know if she comes back or my first patient arrives."

While pacing, Bree found John's name in her contact list and called him.

He answered on the first ring. "Has she shown up at the clinic, Bree?"

"No. I was going to ask you if she has shown up there."

"No, and she hasn't called. I can't get hold of her. This isn't like her. You know how punctual Gail is. She's obsessive about it. She should have been here half an hour ago. I could get a ride home from a buddy leaving in fifteen minutes. If she hasn't come by then, I'll leave and let her know by text. But if you hear anything, please let me know."

"Same for you."

When she punched the off button, she looked out her window at the parking lot where her car had been parked. She began making calls to a patrol officer she knew and then the hospital. Gail hadn't been brought in to any hospital, nor had any officers been dispatched to a wreck involving Bree's Malibu. At least Gail wasn't injured. Relieved, Bree leaned against her desk.

But if she wasn't hurt, then, where was she?

After several hours searching for the child, David returned to Anchorage, taxiing into the hangar at the airport. Ella stood in the doorway of the Northern Frontier office. Weary but glad the little boy had been found, he exited his Cessna, looking forward to a relaxing night. That was, if Bree agreed to stay at his house. Then maybe he could get some quality sleep.

"Bree called a couple of times," Ella said to him. "I told her I'd have you call the second you came back."

He stepped into the warmth of the reception area. "Is something wrong?"

"I don't know, but she sounded stressed."

He strode to his office in the back, sank into his chair, then made a call to Bree. Every muscle tensed. She knew he was on a search and that he would call her when he returned. So why the urgency? As he listened to her phone ringing, a bad feeling gripped him.

"David, I'm so glad you're okay," Bree said the second she answered.

"Of course, the search was pretty routine, and we found the child within an hour. He hadn't wandered too far from town."

"Gail's missing."

"When? What happened?" His hand clutched his cell phone so tightly he had to make himself loosen his grasp.

"She borrowed my car to pick up her husband and do a couple of errands at lunch. She never arrived at the base to get John. Thomas is coming to the clinic because they found my car in the parking lot of the market but no sign of Gail. Five hours after she left for lunch."

"I'll be at the clinic soon. Ask Thomas to stay until I get there."

"Thanks. I'm so glad you're back."

Her words—almost desperate sounding—unnerved him. His protective instinct flowed through him. He wouldn't let anything happen to Bree. "I'm fine, and you will be, too. They'll find Gail." Why did he say that when he couldn't shake his bad feeling?

"I pray you're right." Her sentence ended on a sob.

David shoved to his feet and pocketed his cell phone. As he passed through the reception area, he said to Ella, "Go home. It's nearly six."

"I got the impression something was wrong. No need to round up volunteers to search for someone?"

"Not at this time. If so, I'll take care of it. You've put in a long day."

Ella gathered up her purse and coat. "If you need me, call."

David left with Ella and followed her car from the hangar. At least it wasn't snowing if Thomas wanted to conduct a search for Gail. As he drove toward the clinic, he mentally ran through the handler and dog teams he could call since the scope of the search would be in Anchorage.

When he entered the clinic fifteen minutes later, the first thing he saw was Bree standing with Thomas. Tears ran down her pale face.

EIGHT

David's heart sank at the sight of Bree crying. A tightness expanded in his chest and squeezed the breath from his lungs. He hurried to her, praying he was wrong and the tears were a result of relief.

"I'm glad you're here," Bree said and went into his arms, winding hers around him and holding him close.

David looked at Thomas. "What happened?"

His friend scowled. "We've towed Bree's car in, and it's being processed. We found some blood on the driver's seat. We'll see if it matches Gail's blood type. But at the moment we assume it does, and there has been foul play. We're treating this as a kidnapping. My partner is with the husband. We brought in a dog to see if the abductor left a trail. It led a few feet away, then ended as if she'd been forced into another vehicle."

"Any video surveillance footage of the kidnapping?" David asked as Bree pulled back and pivoted toward Thomas.

"The one in the parking lot isn't working. I have officers checking with the businesses, and we're putting a picture of the car and Gail on the news to see if anyone saw the abduction."

"It was the middle of the day in broad daylight. Surely someone did." Bree wiped wet tracks from her cheeks.

"We hope, but I think the person parked next to the car and waited for her to come back out after shopping. We found a bag on the front seat and the market confirmed she had made some purchases. The problem is that Gail parked near the end of a lane, so if someone had been next to her, it wouldn't be obvious if she didn't fight or scream."

"Gail would have fought." Bree curled her hands, then uncurled them.

"Not if he got to her fast." Thomas started for the door. "I'll keep you informed as the case develops."

A chilling thought nagged David. Before his friend left, he said, "Gail's hair is about the same length and blond like Bree. They are similar in height and build. Gail was driving Bree's car. Could the kidnapper have made a mistake and taken the wrong woman?"

Thomas stopped and glanced back. "A case

of mistaken identity? It's possible. Bree, until we know more, you shouldn't stay at your house alone. If you have somewhere you can go, that might be better."

David opened his mouth to say she did, but Bree cut in first. "Yes, I'm staying at David's. His father is visiting, and he used to be a police officer."

Thomas nodded his head. "Good. Then I'll contact you there."

David moved a couple of feet to Bree and clasped her shoulders from behind. When the detective left, she slumped against him, her body trembling. Fear held him still for a few seconds. Then he bent toward her ear and whispered, "Gail will be found. In the meantime, I'll protect you. I didn't rescue you so you could be hurt." He turned her toward him, worried more than he wanted to admit to Bree.

"If Gail was taken because of me, I'll never be able to forgive myself. First Jeremiah and now possibly Gail. I don't know..." She pressed her lips together, blinking away the returning tears.

He saw the fight for control waged on Bree's face. *She's an innocent having to deal with something out of her control. Why, Lord? What has she done to deserve this?* Anger swelled in David. He'd asked that question many times while serving his country. And now while heading up the SAR organization. Maybe he hadn't chosen the right vocation after retiring from the air force.

He pushed those thoughts away. Bree needed him right now. Drawing her against him, he felt her shudder, but she nestled closer. "You aren't at fault. You did nothing wrong. Jeremiah died of natural causes. Gail borrowed your car. You were being a good friend and helping her out. And it's possible Gail's disappearance has nothing to do with you. The police don't know."

She leaned away. "Why did you mention the similarities between us? And why did Thomas tell me not to be alone, to leave my house?"

"A precaution only. You know the saying, better safe than sorry." He tried to grin, although he wasn't too sure how successful he was. "Besides, you're going to need a chauffeur until the police return your car because you promised me no more skiing to work."

"And you're volunteering?"

"Yes, ma'am. I'm at your service, and if I have to be gone, I offer my dad's service."

"Without asking him?"

"I know him. He'd be the first to step forward."

"Still, I'd feel better if you ask him first."

He ran his hands up and down her arms. "I

will just as soon as we go by your house and you pack a bag."

Bree gathered her purse and coat, then said goodbye to the rest of the staff that had kept a respectable distance. Each one's face reflected concern and worry.

When David pulled into her driveway, a chill streaked down his spine. He stared at Jeremiah's place, then Bree's.

"I left my front blinds open when I went to work. Ringo likes to sun himself when we have sunlight. Someone's closed them," Bree said in a monotone as though she'd had one too many shocks in a single day.

"I'm calling Thomas. I could go check, but I don't want to leave you alone, and I don't want you going in if it's not safe."

When Bree finally entered her house after Thomas and a police officer had gone through it and cleared it, she didn't think she was capable of reacting or feeling. But then she saw the same chaos throughout her place as in Jeremiah's, and it hit her as if she'd been slammed into the side of a mountain.

She stopped at the entrance to her living room and stared, but she really didn't see much. Her mind shut down, and she finally closed her eyes. From behind, David wrapped his arms around her. She knew it was him from the sense of safety that suffused her and his distinctive scent that was becoming familiar to her.

"Let's get some clothes for you and then leave. We can deal with this mess tomorrow."

His softly spoken words washed over her, and for a moment she felt at peace as if God had sent David to help her. She wasn't alone. She nodded, then turned within the circle of his arms, her gaze fixed only on him. "This isn't important. Only Gail is right now."

She picked her way through the disarray on her floor without even noting what it was and entered her bedroom, keeping her focus on finding some clothes and then leaving. While David positioned himself in the doorway, she zeroed in on one item after another tossed on the floor, blocking everything else from her consciousness, until she had what she needed for a few days.

Ten minutes later, holding one duffel bag stuffed with her possessions, she faced Thomas in the foyer. Her attention strayed to the living room and her pulse rate accelerated when she noticed the cushion seats on the couch, cut open and torn apart. Squeezing her eyes closed, she lowered her head, then slowly opened them to see the relatively clean entry hall.

David slipped his arm around her shoulders

while he took her duffel bag. "She'll be at my house," he reminded Thomas. "Either my dad or I will be with her until you figure out what's going on."

"Good. This time we found footprints leading from the back door to the woods behind this house. I have two officers following them right now. I imagine, though, they'll end when they reach tire tracks."

"Please let me know whatever you find concerning Gail. I…" Bree cleared her throat, but no words came to mind to say.

"I will, Bree. We'll be processing your house. Maybe we'll find some evidence that will lead us to who is behind this."

A loud whine filled the air. Bree covered her mouth and turned toward David. "I forgot about Ringo. How could I?"

"You've had a lot to deal with. Here, take your bag. I'll find him. We can stop by the store to get what he needs."

"You don't mind taking him to your house?"

"I love animals. It's about time I have one at my place. Remember I volunteered to take him when you're at a village clinic." David went to retrieve the cat.

Thomas waited with her. "He's a good guy. You're in good hands. I wish we had the manpower to protect you, but we don't."

"I still don't understand why someone would search my house. I don't have any of Jeremiah's possessions over here except Ringo, and he's just a stray cat Jeremiah took in a few years ago."

"If we knew what they were looking for, we might know what's going on and put a stop to it."

Bree studied Thomas's face. "I know you still feel this is about drugs. It isn't."

The police detective remained quiet.

David returned to the foyer, holding a crying and wiggling cat. Bree set her bag on the floor and took Ringo into her arms. He began rubbing against her cheek and his whining stopped.

"Let's go." David grabbed her duffel and opened the front door.

As Bree left her house, she glanced back over her shoulder and realized her home mirrored her life—turned upside down and shattered into pieces.

Early the next morning, after finding Ringo standing over him on his bed, David threw on a pair of jeans and a sweatshirt and headed for the kitchen to make coffee. The quiet of his house soothed his raw nerves from the intensity of the past week. At the end of the hall, he peered back at his bedroom and wondered how

Ringo had ended up there. He'd closed his door last night when he'd gone to sleep, but obviously not totally.

The cat followed him into the kitchen, purring and rubbing against David's jeans. He checked to make sure Ringo's water bowl was full, then went to the counter to fix a pot of coffee.

David knew someone was in the entrance before he heard a sound. He turned. His father ambled into the room.

"Good morning, son. Did you sleep last night?"

"Yes."

"How long?"

"Not long. A couple of hours."

His dad took down two mugs from the cabinet and slid them toward David. "Me, neither. Every sound had me going for my gun. I haven't guarded a person in years."

"I appreciate you helping me. Maybe we should take turns so we can get some sleep."

"That's a good suggestion, and one I should have come up with last night. I shouldn't be surprised by the turn of events, but when it is someone you know, it's hard to think of everything you should do. Emotions get in the way of clear thinking."

David filled each mug and gave his dad his coffee. "You like Bree."

Although not a question, his father said, "Yes. She's open and easy to like, but I do think she might be blind about her friend Jeremiah."

"I hope not. It'll shatter her, especially after what has happened with Gail."

"The longer Gail is gone, the less her chances are of being alive. There hasn't been a ransom demand, which means something else besides money is the motive for taking her. Money is easier to deal with."

Sipping his drink, David leaned back against the counter and crossed his ankles. "I'm worried about Bree, especially if the police find Gail dead."

"Perhaps you more than like her."

"I like her, but that is all." He had to put a stop to the feelings developing between them. "After Trish, I'm not ready to jump back into a relationship. I made a mess of that one."

"When she married you, she knew you'd made a commitment to your country. Your life is different now. You have more freedom of time and choices than you had before."

"I've enjoyed this past year with Northern Frontier, but I'm not sure what I want to do with the rest of my life."

"You'll figure that out. Make sure it's something you love. God made us for a purpose. Discover yours." His father went to the refrigerator and pulled out some ingredients. "Do you know if Bree is going into work?"

"I'm not," Bree said from the doorway, holding Ringo in her arms. "I asked for the next few weeks off. I can't put any more people in jeopardy. I hate even putting you two in danger. If something happens to—"

His dad cut her off. "Stop right there, young lady. It wasn't that long ago I was protecting a whole town from the bad guys. I think protecting one woman is much safer." His dad put the container of eggs on the counter beside the refrigerator. He looked pointedly at David, then crossed the room. "I have a few calls to make, then I'll cook something for breakfast."

When his father left, the silence between David and Bree separated them more than the width of the kitchen did. He was at a loss for words. She was worried about him and his dad, while all he thought about was keeping her safe at any cost. When had his feelings shifted from more than friendship? He still wasn't ready for any kind of serious relationship, and yet there was no way he would ask her to leave because he was beginning to care for her. If anything happened to her, he would never forgive himself.

"Do you want some coffee?" he asked after several minutes passed.

She released Ringo, then finally answered, "Yes, please."

He poured her some and passed it to her. "Let's sit and talk. I want to emphasize that my dad is right. You belong here."

While Ringo sauntered to his empty bowl and licked it as if food would somehow appear for him, Bree went into the utility room and retrieved his food bag. After feeding the cat, she came to the table and took a seat across from David.

"Ringo is definitely taking this better than me. He's acting like he's been here for years." Bree ran her finger around the rim of the mug, studying it intently. "I feel so alone. I can't shake the feeling I'm responsible for Gail's disappearance." She looked up at him. "If this isn't settled by the time Melissa comes for Christmas, I'm leaving. I won't put her in danger and nothing you say will change my mind."

He captured her hand and cupped it between his. "We have time. Don't think about that now. Thomas is a friend, and he'll do all he can to solve this case. I do think you were wise to take a few weeks off, though."

"The hard part of taking off is I like to be kept busy. It feels strange to have that much time off. Whenever I take a vacation, it's only for a week at a time."

"I'll be with you. Ella will contact me if I need to know about any operation that comes up. Otherwise, I'm at your disposal. Chauffeur and friend, all wrapped up in one person."

"Good. I'm in need of both." Her look embraced him. "Today I'm supposed to go see Jeremiah's lawyer. Then I want to visit John, Gail's husband."

"Are you sure about that?"

"Yes. She's a good friend, and he needs to know I'm here for him."

"What time is your appointment with the lawyer?"

"Eleven. John…and Gail live on the outskirts of Anchorage."

David rose. "More coffee?"

She shook her head.

"Does he know you're coming this afternoon?"

"No. I realize he might not be there, but I'm afraid if I tell him, he'll say I shouldn't come. I have to talk to him in person. Let him know I'm praying for Gail's safe return."

"Do you think that will do any good?" The second he asked the question, he wanted to take it back.

"Yes. I can't even begin to tell you what God's plan is for me or anyone else, but at least I can let Him know what I want. If I don't have Him, what kind of hope do I have?"

"I used to think that, but after so many prayers went unanswered, I'm beginning to feel He isn't listening to me. Maybe He is for you."

"I know He's listening, but that doesn't mean He'll grant every wish and prayer a person has. He sees the bigger picture. I don't. Part of having faith is believing through the good and bad. My faith is what keeps me going through the bad times. He's with me."

"During my last two tours of duty, I felt my prayers were falling on deaf ears. People were dying. People there lived in horrific situations. And nothing I did seemed to change anything."

"That's because we aren't in control. Never have been. I have the most difficulties when I try to control my life. When I try to do things by myself, it often becomes a struggle. I'm trying right now to turn this over to the Lord. It should be easy, but it isn't. I want to be out there searching for Gail. The least I can do is talk to John."

David released a long breath. "I've been wrestling with my faith for years. I've lost touch with God."

"I've felt that at times. But if I close myself off when I'm struggling, who can I turn to?"

"You said earlier you feel all alone."

"I am alone and grasping on to my faith. We

were never guaranteed an easy life, but God did say He would be with us through that life—the good and bad times. But I can forget that when something awful occurs, like Gail's disappearance. I wonder where God is in all of this."

"Are you two hungry?" his dad called in a loud voice from the hallway.

David bent forward and whispered, "Sometimes he isn't too subtle."

"What's that about?"

"Earlier he told me you were good for me, that it was time that I move on with my life." *Why did I say that? That implies I'm looking and I'm not.*

Red shaded Bree's cheeks as his father came into the kitchen. She averted her head and smiled at his dad. "I'm starved."

"One big breakfast coming up then."

While Bree engaged in a conversation with his father, David relaxed back in his chair and thought about what she'd said about having faith even when the bad things happen. *Does she really believe that? Can I have that kind of faith?* What was going on right now certainly wasn't working.

"Everything was left to me?" Bree asked as the lawyer finished going over the will.

"Yes, the house, the possessions in it, his

plane, which I understand is wrecked and missing, his Jeep, any money he has, a small life insurance policy and his cabin."

Stunned, Bree tried to assimilate what Jeremiah's lawyer had rattled off. "I didn't know he had a cabin. Where is it?"

"I don't know that. He recently purchased one and had me add it to his will. He didn't want there to be any doubt he wanted you to have it." Mr. Anderson opened a drawer and removed a letter. "I was also to give you this letter upon his death. I think this will explain everything. At least he told me it would." He handed the envelope to her. "When is his funeral?" the lawyer asked.

"His body was just released for burial, and I'm planning a memorial service at the church I go to—First Community Church. I'll be finalizing arrangements tomorrow morning."

"Thanks. Jeremiah was my client but a friend, too. He helped so many people who needed it. He used me to send money when he discovered someone in need."

Tears threatened her composure once again. Mr. Anderson was confirming what she'd always known about Jeremiah—his kind heart, especially for the underdog. "I will miss him. If you know of anyone in trouble that Jeremiah would help, please let me know. I'll be selling his house, and I can use that money to continue doing what he did."

"Fine." The lawyer drew the word out, then added, "If you want to read the letter in private, I can leave for a few minutes."

"No. I'll read it later."

Mr. Anderson rose and extended his hand. "He's smiling down at us."

Standing, Bree shook it. "At least his death was sudden, and he didn't suffer much. That's a comfort. He always hated a big fuss. I'm not even sure he would approve of having a memorial service, but I think his friends should have a chance to say goodbye."

"Most definitely. Closure is so important for the ones left behind. I'll keep you informed as the estate goes through probate."

"Thank you."

As Bree left the lawyer's office, the moment was bittersweet. The man reinforced everything good that she knew about Jeremiah. But she so wished she hadn't had to come today.

David came to his feet, giving her a reassuring smile as she crossed the reception area. "Are you okay?"

"I will be once I can get back to my normal, dull life. Jeremiah wrote me a letter to be read on his death. I'll look at it in the car on the way to John and Gail's."

David walked beside her down the long first-floor hall of the professional building in downtown Anchorage. When she emerged outside, the sun brightened the day, and for a few seconds, its light lifted her spirits as though the Lord was showering her with His brilliance.

Everything will be all right. She latched on to that thought and hurried toward David's Jeep. When she settled into the passenger seat and David pulled out of the parking space, she slowly opened the letter, wanting to savor the last contact she'd have with Jeremiah. She'd thought about waiting and reading it later in the guest bedroom at David's, but she couldn't.

As she read the letter, her jaw dropped. The trembling started in her hands and quickly spread throughout her body. She nearly let the piece of paper go.

"What's wrong?" David asked at a stoplight.

"Jeremiah wants me to go to a bank where he opened a safety-deposit box. My name is on it, too. He said directions to his cabin are in the box, along with some other stuff he wants me to have." She held up the safety-deposit box's key.

"Cabin? He has one?"

"Apparently so, recently. I didn't know about it, and he never said anything about buying one. I don't know where he got the money for it. He was always scrimping by." Bree turned toward

David. "Mr. Anderson said Jeremiah often helped others out financially, so I guess that's where his money went. He never said a word about that, but that doesn't surprise me because he was always doing things for me without me knowing. Once I came back from my month's rotation at a village to find my house had been painted outside. He'd known I wanted to do it and had planned on doing it when I returned to Anchorage."

"That's a nice surprise."

"Yes, especially because I wasn't expecting it. I've been saving my money to pay off my college loans and was going to do it myself. Now do you see why I don't think Jeremiah could have anything to do with selling drugs?"

"I agree, but something is going on with all that has happened in the past week."

Bree drew in a fortifying breath. "I know. Let's visit the bank before going to John and Gail's." She gave him the name and address, pressing the key to the box into her palm as if that made the whole experience real.

He made a turn at the next corner and headed back the way they had come. Fifteen minutes later, Bree waited until the bank teller left the room to open the safety-deposit box. David lounged against the door with his arms and legs crossed.

Slowly Bree lifted the lid on the box and gasped at the sight before her.

NINE

As the sound of the lid clanging down on the box echoed through the small room, David shoved off the door and was at Bree's side in seconds. "What's wrong?"

Bree's hands shook as she opened it again. "Look at this. Where did this come from?"

A Eurobond sat on top of a stack of papers. David picked it up and another one was beneath it. He counted ten Eurobonds in all. "At the current rate, these are worth over a million dollars."

"How do you know? Where did Jeremiah get this kind of money?"

"I have some investments overseas and keep track of that kind of thing. These bonds are like bearer bonds in the United States."

"Jeremiah never seemed interested in the stock market or anything like that."

Below the Eurobonds was an envelope with Bree's name on it. "Maybe this will explain where the bonds came from." He pushed away the thought of drug running as a source, but that left the question: Where did Jeremiah get the money?

Bree tore into the envelope and read out loud, "Years ago your father helped me buy my first plane. I'm repaying the debt plus interest. He would never take the money from me, but I didn't want to die without fulfilling that obligation. Below are the directions to a cabin I purchased. Another dream your dad and I had—to escape into the wilderness and live off the land when we grew old and retired." Bree glanced at David. "I didn't know Dad helped him buy his first plane. I do remember Dad talking about a cabin with Mom and Jeremiah."

David laid the bonds in the box. "He repaid your dad plus interest and then some."

She stared at the certificates, touching the top one. "I guess I didn't really know Jeremiah."

"What else does he say?"

Bree returned her attention to the letter and continued, "It's where I go to retreat from life. You'll love the cabin. So would your parents have, and my regret is that I didn't buy it sooner. I hope you can use it when you need to get away. You were the daughter I never had. I love you. Jeremiah." Holding up the piece of paper, she cleared her throat. "These are the coordinates of the cabin at the bottom of the letter, and also I believe this is the key for it." She held it up.

"Do you want to go and see it?"

Bree blinked several times as though fighting tears. "I don't know what I want or should do." She slammed the lid closed on the safety-deposit box. "For the time being, I'm leaving the bonds here, and I'll tell Mr. Anderson about them since they're part of the estate. I can't deal with it now."

He saw fear in her eyes as she raised them to his. "Are you concerned about where this money might have come from?"

Silent, Bree bit her lower lip. Finally she nodded. "It scares me what I'm finding out about Jeremiah. I loved him. He was always there for me, but he must have lived a secret life." She waved her hand at the box. "If it was obtained legitimately, then why keep it a secret?" Slumping against the counter, she gripped its edge. "If I could misread him so much, how can I ever trust my perceptions of others again?"

"There are times I've wondered that, too. When I left my wife to go on assignment in the Middle East, she told me she was fine and urged me to go. I thought she was." Even though he was surprised he'd told Bree that much, he couldn't stop the flow of words once he started. "I should have known she wasn't and alerted someone. Done something to save her. Trish put on a front, and I let her because I was focused on the upcoming mission. In the end she over-dosed. I have to live with that guilt."

"Guilt has a way of attacking a person even years later. My fiancé was killed in an accident because I challenged him to a downhill race. We were always competitive and doing things like that. At least that's what I tell myself when guilt raises its ugly head and stops me in my tracks. I'm already regretting having Jeremiah come pick me up the day he had his heart attack. If only I hadn't, he might be alive because he could have gotten the help he needed in time. I couldn't save him."

David grasped her hands and held them, moving nearer to her. "We're a pair. The what-ifs in life really can be damaging to a person's peace."

"God doesn't want us reliving our past but to live for the present. Learn from the past mistakes but don't let them cripple you. You know who told me that? Gail."

David gathered her to him and held her. Her presence in his embrace soothed the memories their conversation produced. He had regrets about his marriage, ones he wished he could redo. But that wasn't possible. He needed to move on. And he wanted to help Bree see that she should, too.

She gave him a squeeze, then stepped back, her glance straying to the safety-deposit box. A shudder passed through her. "I need to get out of here."

"Let's go grab some lunch—then we can head to John's."

As David escorted Bree to his Jeep, he marveled at how easy she was to talk to. He'd told her things he didn't share with others. If only he could talk about his last tour of duty...

As Bree approached her friend's porch, her heart raced. If Gail had been kidnapped because she was in Bree's car... She should have been the one taken. How could she tell that to John? Her step faltered, and she slowed her pace, trying to gather her courage and composure to be there for John.

David touched the small of her back and moved closer. "You are not at fault. Only the person who took Gail. Don't talk yourself into it."

She paused at the bottom of the stairs. "I don't have to. I already feel that way."

"You were helping a friend. We don't know what's going to happen in the future. Remember that."

A part of her knew what David was saying was true, but she couldn't shake the other part that heaped more guilt on her. "Thanks for being with me, or I'm not sure I would be brave enough to come."

David scoffed at the words. "You? Not brave? A lady who fought off a pack of wolves. Kept her wits about her and remained alive in a snowstorm after a wreck. You can't convince me you aren't brave."

A smile graced her mouth for a second. Until the door opened and she peered at John standing in the entrance. Bree stiffened.

John stepped out on the porch. "I'm glad you came. I've been worried about you."

She nearly crumbled at the sincerity in his voice. David slipped his arm around her waist.

"Don't just stand there. C'mon in. It's freezing out here." John reentered his house.

Bree followed him inside with David behind her. "John, this is David Stone. He is the pilot who rescued me last week."

"Nice to meet you," John said as he shook David's hand. Then he turned back to Bree. "I tried your house and the clinic. I couldn't find your cell phone number. The receptionist said you're taking the next few weeks off."

"I can't let anything happen to anyone else. David and his father are—" she looked back at him "—my protectors. The police detective working the case didn't think I should be alone."

She met John's gaze. "They aren't ruling out the possibility I was the target, not Gail."

"I was told that this morning when Detective Thomas Caldwell came by, but he also said that they are looking into Gail's life. They wanted to know if she had problems with anyone lately." John clasped his arms across his chest. "I honestly couldn't think of a soul. They wondered about problems that might have arisen at the clinic. Gail never said anything to me."

"There wasn't any problem that I know of, but I've just come back from being gone for a month. I know the detective was talking to everyone at work."

"Come in and sit. I want to make sure you're all right. That's why I called this morning." John sank into a chair across from the couch where Bree and David sat.

Bree swallowed to coat her dry throat, then said, "I'm trying to understand what's going on. I can't think of anyone who would do this to Gail or me."

"It's possible it could be a predator, that Gail was snatched at random. If so…" A tic jerked in John's cheek. "If so…" He shook his head and averted his gaze. "I have to leave this in God's hands. I feel so helpless."

As do I. Bree stood and moved to John, then knelt next to him. "If there's anything I can do,

I will. Would you like me to bring you some food?" She touched his arm, hoping to convey how much she cared for him and Gail.

"No. The people at the base and church have been bringing food by. My sister just went home to pack a bag. She's staying with me. Praying is all I can ask of you. That and to keep yourself safe."

"I'll make sure she is," David said.

John placed his hand over hers. "Thank you for coming. I needed to see that you were all right."

The finality in his words indicated he wanted to be alone. She'd known Gail and John for three years and cherished their friendship. "If you need anything, please let me know." She rose and grabbed her purse, then wrote her cell phone number on a receipt. "You can call me anytime you need someone to talk to."

John nodded.

"We can find our way out." Bree headed toward the foyer, her heart breaking at the pain etched on John's face and in his voice.

Outside she drew in a deep inhalation of the frigid air. "I'm glad we came, but that was tough. At least his sister is staying with him. He doesn't need to be alone for long."

"When we get back to my house, I'm calling Thomas. Maybe something has developed today."

"If it had, he'd have called."

"I know. But this inactivity is driving me crazy. Besides, he needs to know about the bonds and cabin."

"He's going to think Jeremiah was into something illegal unless Mr. Anderson knows differently. Nothing we found at Jeremiah's house explains the large amount of money. Could he have stolen the bonds?" She finally asked out loud what she'd been wondering since she opened the safety-deposit box.

"We may never know. The United States doesn't issue bearer bonds anymore that allow whoever brings them to a bank to cash them in. There was trouble with people hiding and stealing money. Eurobonds are more like what US bonds used to be."

Bree climbed into his car while David rounded the hood and slid behind the steering wheel. "Maybe we should go back and search Jeremiah's house again."

"Did he have any hidey-holes in his house?" David asked as he backed out of the driveway.

"If he did, I didn't know about them, but that doesn't mean anything because obviously I didn't know a lot about Jeremiah."

Bree took in the landscape around them and the absence of homes in the area. Off through the trees, she spied a light from one house and another down the road, but that was all. Suddenly a chill shook her insides. While they had been inside talking with John, the sun had set and it had grown dark. Not far behind them she noticed headlights as a car pulled onto the road and followed them.

"Where did that car come from?" she asked, trying to think of what they had passed. All she remembered were trees. Maybe a dirt path? A house back behind the woods?

"I've got an eye on it." David accelerated as much as he could on the snow-packed pavement.

Bree's pulse rate increased, as well. Then in the distance coming toward them was another pair of headlights. She breathed a little easier. They weren't alone. She hated this feeling of being paranoid, but after what had happened to Gail, anything was possible. If the abductors were after her, she was sure they'd realized Gail wasn't her by now.

The vehicle behind them picked up speed while the one in front slowed down. Bree gripped the door handle.

"You've got your seat belt on, don't you?" David asked in a tight voice.

"Yes," she squeaked out as the car in front swerved across the road at the last minute, blocking them.

David braked but drove the SUV toward the side of the highway.

The headlights behind them were coming fast.

"Hang on."

David plowed his vehicle through half a foot of snow on the shoulder, his rear end fishtailing. But he kept going, even gunning the SUV as the front wheels bounced back onto the road.

Bree turned around and looked out the rear window. The car blocking their path backed up and fell in behind the other one, still coming toward them.

"Call nine-one-one, then Thomas," David said and gave her his phone number. "Tell him where we are and what's happening."

After she disconnected with 911, she called Thomas, who answered on the second ring. She looked around and told him where they were and what was happening. "These guys may be who took Gail."

Thomas explained where they would try to set up a roadblock. "Hang in there."

As Bree ended the call, David pressed down on the accelerator. She glanced behind them at the two sets of headlights still following, with the lead car gaining on them. "Thomas wants you to get to Otter Road and stay on it."

"I want to catch these guys." David's fierce tone cut through the charged air.

Although David slowed for a big curve, the SUV began to glide toward the shoulder. He steered into the slide and managed to right the car. Bree kept her attention focused on the two vehicles behind them. One hit the curve at a high speed and flew off the side of the road into a ditch. The second one decelerated in time and continued pursuing them.

"One down," Bree said. "Let's hope he stays that way."

"He isn't getting out of that ravine. I noticed it on the way to John's. It's four or five feet deep. The car will have to be towed."

His words comforted Bree until she noticed the vehicle still behind them was recklessly cutting the distance between them. "I don't think the one left is too concerned about ending up in a ditch."

"Otter Road is up ahead. Let's hope Thomas has everything ready."

"I'm so sorry you're going through this because of me. When you rescued me from the wreck, you weren't counting on this."

"When does anyone know what the future holds?"

David took the turn as fast as he could and still control his Jeep. The vehicle behind them kept coming like a polar bear stalking its prey. Bree clasped her hands together so tightly her fingers ached. She couldn't be responsible for David's life. *Please, God, deliver us safely.* She repeated it over and over.

The cell phone rang in Bree's lap. She noticed it was Thomas calling and snatched it up. "Is the roadblock set up?"

"Yes," he said, then told her the location. "There's a curve, so once David passes, we will be putting out the spikes to stop the car behind him."

"Thanks. We're not too far from there, but the guy after us is daring. He keeps pushing the speed." When she disconnected, she told David the roadblock's location.

"That's another mile."

When David went around the curve, Bree spied the highway patrol on both sides of the road. After they passed, the officers threw out the chain of spikes to stop the pursuing car.

"I'm not slowing until we get to my house."

Bree turned to watch as the vehicle plowed over the spike chain. The driver lost control when his tires blew out. He tried to keep going but didn't get very far. The highway patrol officers surrounded the car, guns drawn.

David let out a long breath. "Call Thomas and hand me the cell phone."

Bree did. Then, with one last look behind them, she relaxed back against the cushion, exhaustion blanketing her. If there had ever been any doubt that she was the target rather than Gail, the past twenty minutes had erased it.

The next morning, David sat in his living room checking his emails, drinking this third cup of coffee. He looked up as his dad entered. "Did you sleep okay?" His father had complained of insomnia the past few nights.

"Better. I'm not responding to every sound I hear."

"Good. That means you feel safe enough to sleep while I'm on guard duty."

"Do you want a coffee refill? I'm going to get me one."

David shook his head and finished up his last email, then closed his laptop. He wasn't looking forward to the day with Jeremiah's memorial service. Every time Bree left his house, he felt there was a target on her back, especially after the direct assault while returning from John's.

"I assume Bree is still asleep," his dad said when he returned from the kitchen with his mug full.

"Yes, and I'm glad because she is another one who hasn't been sleeping. After what happened last evening, she probably fell into bed and was out instantly."

"Has Thomas called yet about the man they captured? I hope they were able to get some information out of him last night."

"Not yet. He told me he would be over later and fill us in. He'll also be at the memorial service with several patrol officers."

"Did you figure out where Jeremiah's cabin is?" His father sipped his coffee.

"Yes. I plotted the coordinates on the map and have the location."

"Maybe we should go there for a while. If Bree didn't know about the cabin, I don't see how anyone else would." His father took a seat across from David.

"I've been thinking about that. I feel like we're sitting ducks here. We could let Thomas know where we're going but no one else. I'm sure there's a place to land a plane nearby. That would have been important to Jeremiah."

"Let's see what Bree says."

"About what?" Bree came into the living room, dressed in jeans and a sweatshirt from the University of Alaska.

"We thought it might be good to get away from Anchorage while Thomas tracks down any leads from last night."

"What leads?" She eased onto the other end of the couch from David, then angled toward him.

"I don't know yet. I'm thinking positively since they caught one of the people after us. That was more than we had this time yesterday."

"True. Where can we go?"

"To Jeremiah's cabin."

"You know where it is?"

David rose, went to the dining room table and grabbed the map he'd plotted the location on, then spread it out on the coffee table before the couch. "Here." He tapped his finger on the general spot on a stream with a forest surrounding it.

Bree's face took on a thoughtful look. Her eyes narrowed, and she studied the map. "You know, I think I've been there…maybe."

"What do you mean? When?" His dad joined them.

"We flew over this general area, and he came down along a stream like this one. Jeremiah said he had some Christmas presents to drop off at a friend's cabin. He took a bag, and I saw some wrapped gifts in it. He didn't stay long and then we took off. It wasn't long after that he had his heart attack and landed on the lake."

David caught his father's glance. "Are you thinking what I'm thinking?"

"Maybe something was in the bag of presents those people want," his father said.

David nodded.

Bree straightened. "You two think so?"

"It's a good place to start looking. You couldn't find anything at Jeremiah's house, and his Jeep is missing from his parking space at the airport. But since Gail was taken after that and you two nearly were last night, I don't think they found what they want." His father went back to his chair and sat. "We should plan to stay for a while. That way we can search the cabin and have a hideaway."

"But no one should know where. We'll tell Thomas we're going into hiding and will keep in touch by satellite phone. I have one I use with my search and rescues." David studied Bree, who appeared more rested. After arriving home last night, she'd prowled the house, constantly peeking out the blinds until finally the need for sleep overtook her apprehension. "Are you okay with this, Bree?"

"Yes. I'm curious about the cabin and those packages. If it is Jeremiah's place, he probably lied to me when he told me he was dropping off the presents at a friend's. Obviously that wasn't his first lie to me."

Her look of sadness pinned David to the couch. He wanted to comfort Bree, to wipe away all the bad memories of late, but he couldn't. He sensed her building a wall between them, as though that would protect her. Jeremiah had hurt her, and she was slowly coming to realize that. He knew what that felt like. Trish had done the same thing to him.

"We'll get to the bottom of this," he told her.

When the doorbell rang, his father pushed to his feet to answer it. "That's probably Thomas— I hope with good news."

Bree captured David's gaze. "Do you think that's possible?"

"Possible, yes. Likely, no."

"Why do you say that?"

"Just a gut feeling. Those men in the two cars weren't the people behind all of this. I think something big is going on, and they're just cogs in the wheel, doing what they are told."

A weary Thomas moved into the room, his pace slow, his shoulders drooping. "I wish I had good news for you, but Bruce Keller, the guy driving the car we nabbed at the roadblock, isn't saying a word. He lawyered up instantly. We've come to find out he's a known hired gun who has had a few brushes with the police. I'll be interviewing him later after he meets with his attorney. Maybe I'll have something when I see you at the memorial service at two."

"How about the driver and car in the ditch?"

David asked as his dad took his mug and headed for the kitchen.

"He was gone when we arrived, but we have fingerprints in the stolen vehicle, and they're in the system. Another hired gun. This morning I'll be tracking down Sonny Franks. He has some ties to a drug gang."

"Do you have a photo of both men?" David slanted a look at Bree, who tensed and frowned at Thomas.

"Yes." He slipped two pictures out of his pocket and passed them to David.

After examining them, he gave them to Bree. "Have you seen either one of them?"

While staring at the top photo, her frown deepened and her eyes darkened. "I saw him the morning my duffel bag was left at work. He was at the end of the alleyway behind the clinic. People loiter there sometimes, so I didn't think much about it." She set it on the coffee table in front of her. "So it's possible he's the one who left it at the back door."

"We'll ask Sonny Franks when we find him. I have a BOLO out on him, and his parole officer is checking around, too. I came from Keller's apartment, hoping to find something to indicate where Gail might be. Nothing other than the man is the worst housekeeper and the stench of rotten food turned my stomach." Before David could say it might not be food, Thomas continued, "And I checked to make sure that caused the smell. His dirty dishes were stacked next to the sink, but that was as far as they got to being cleaned."

"I know that David told you what was in Jeremiah's safety-deposit box," Bree said to Thomas, concern evident in her voice. "I didn't realize Jeremiah had that kind of money. I don't know how he would have gotten it. Is there anything you can do to see where all his money came from?"

The look on Bree's face, so full of sadness, made David's heart twist. If he could, he'd erase the past week.

"Maybe. We'll dig into Jeremiah's financial records. With your okay, we can start right away."

His dad reentered the living room with mugs and a coffeepot. He poured and passed the coffee to each person. "Have you told him what we're going to do tomorrow?" he asked David.

Thomas's eyebrows lifted.

Despite already having had too much caffeine, David took a swig of the coffee. "We're leaving for a while. If they don't know where we are, they can't come after us." He held up his hand to Thomas. "Before you say anything, you're the only one we're telling. I'll check in with you each morning and evening. I'm taking my satellite phone. We'll leave before sunrise tomorrow. It's getting too dangerous here."

"Actually that's not a bad idea. I'd like Bree out of Anchorage until we find out what's going on and who's behind it."

Bree sagged against the couch. "Good. I don't want to go on another high-speed chase over icy roads again. Not my idea of fun."

His dad chuckled. "It's right up there with going to the dentist for a root canal."

With her mug in hand, Bree smiled at Don and stood. "If you all will excuse me, I'm going to find a quiet place to come up with what I'll say at the memorial service."

After she left, David said to Thomas, "Make sure you keep Bruce Keller in jail until we get out of town."

"We can, but without more evidence we won't be able to charge him with attempted assault and kidnapping, only reckless driving, and I'm afraid he won't talk, especially with the lawyer he's hired. Keller isn't on parole like Franks, and the car he used was his own. If we catch Franks, we might be able to persuade him to tell us who he's working for."

"Thanks for letting me know. I'll see you later today. In the meantime we'll get ready to leave."

"Be careful. With what has happened, whoever is behind it has money. So far we haven't found the helicopter you described." Thomas finished his coffee. "I need to go. I'll let myself out."

David followed Thomas to the front door. "I've got to lock it anyway."

"Who'll be overseeing Northern Frontier Search and Rescue while you're gone?"

"Ella. She can organize a search if you need one." David shut the door behind Thomas and drew the deadbolt.

Its clicking sound should have reassured him, but if someone wanted to get in badly enough, it was possible, even with good security. Although last night traffic had been light, Keller and Franks had openly come after Bree. Couple that with what had happened to Jeremiah's plane, and someone was desperately looking for...what? Drugs? Something else on the black market?

It didn't make any difference what they wanted. He had to protect Bree. Maybe if he rescued enough people, his guilt would fade.

Bree stepped away from the podium after delivering the last tribute to Jeremiah at his memorial service and retook her seat. One of his friends ended with singing "Amazing Grace," which finally brought tears to Bree, who had battled them all the way through her speech. David, sitting next to her in the front pew, clasped her hand.

Even if Jeremiah had done something illegal, she still loved him and would miss him every day. But it was looking more and more like he had been up to something shady. Thomas was trying to track how Jeremiah ended up with Eurobonds worth about a million dollars in a safety-deposit box. The amount stunned her. She'd never had an idea that Jeremiah had that kind of money. How could she think she knew someone so well and really she didn't?

She looked sideways at David and began to wonder what he was hiding. She was falling in love with him and she couldn't. Right now she needed him, but the second she could, she must put as much space between them as possible or she would end up with a broken heart—again. *I can't take that, Lord. Help me. I know You still are here and love me. I need You.*

When people began to file out of the church to the reception hall, Bree wanted to remain where she was. She didn't know if she could put on a front for Jeremiah's friends and colleagues. At the moment she didn't have it in her.

"Are you ready to go?" David asked when the pews were empty.

Bree glanced at the double glass doors into

the sanctuary. Thomas stood at them with another police officer. "The whole time I was talking about Jeremiah and his life, I kept thinking which part was a lie." She shifted to face David. "And what about Gail? The longer she is missing, the more likely she is dead. We haven't talked about it lately, but I know her chances of being found alive are diminishing each hour. I want to be out there looking for her. I want..." No other words filled her anguish-drenched mind.

David gathered her to him. "I want to be out there searching, too. That's what I do. But right now it's important to keep you alive and find the people behind this. We need to go to the cabin and discover what they must be looking for. That might help us find Gail."

His arms anchored Bree to him. She listened to the beating of his heart and dug deep for her fighting spirit. These people were not going to win. *God is my refuge and strength.* She needed to remember that.

Tears stung her eyes, but she was determined not to release them. There was too much that must be done. She pulled away from David's embrace and rose.

God is my refuge and strength.

"I don't want to stay long at the reception,"

she said. "We need to get ready to leave tomorrow. I wish we could go right now."

"We'll be there by the time the sun rises in the morning." David stood, and, with her beside him, headed for the exit. "We'll stay no more than fifteen minutes. Thomas will be glad when we leave. If he had his way, you wouldn't have come."

"I know, but I owed Jeremiah at least this, even if I'm angry and confused. I still love him." As Bree walked into the reception hall, she wondered why she could forgive Jeremiah for lying to her all these years, but she couldn't forgive herself for Anthony's accident. Why was she holding on to the past?

"This must be it." David flew low along a stream, staring at a cabin set back in the forest of evergreens and bare deciduous trees.

Bree leaned forward and looked out the windshield. "Yes. There's a stretch of ground he used to land on, next to the stream not far from the cabin."

"I see it." David threw a look over his shoulder. "Dad, are you okay back there?"

"I'll be fine once we're on the ground."

"You would think he'd be used to flying with a son who is a pilot. If this wasn't really important, he wouldn't be here." David sent

Bree a smile. "I have a good feeling about this. We'll find what we need, and the people will be caught. Gail will be located alive and well."

"That's what I've been praying for." She turned to David. "It'll be nice to have a change of scenery. I was going stir-crazy in your house. You didn't even show me your workshop in the back."

"I promise I'll give you the grand tour when we aren't worried about someone coming after us." David flew over the spot he would use as a landing strip, then came back around to line up to set his Cessna down. "This is a nice place to land. I wonder if Jeremiah worked on it and cleared some of the bush."

"When it came to his plane, he was very particular, so I wouldn't be surprised if he did."

David glanced at his dad's pale face and white-knuckled grip on the seat. "In a moment you can kiss the ground if you want."

"Bah! Bree, can you believe this guy loves to tease his dad about flying?"

She chuckled. "Yes. We'll have to figure a way to get back at him."

"I like that. Hear that, son? You better watch out."

The plane touched down and came to a smooth stop seconds later. "In case you don't know, we're here." David heard the click of the seat belt as he spoke to his father.

The door opened, and his father scrambled to the ground.

"I'm not sure we're related." David shut down the Cessna.

"How did he get to Alaska?"

"He drove."

Bree pressed her lips together, but laughter danced in her eyes.

"Now you see how monumental this is to have my dad in my plane."

"I'm going to give him an extra hug. With all that has been happening, I would have wanted him to stay back at your house. But what if they had come after him to get to us?"

"Don't tell him that. He thinks he can take care of himself in any situation, and usually he can, but anyone can be overpowered. Ready?"

"Yes, we have a cabin to search." Bree unfastened her seat belt and exited the Cessna.

David followed and opened the cargo bay, then passed their bags to Bree and his dad. David carried the box of provisions through the snow to the porch of the cabin. "It's comforting not to see any footprints."

His dad headed toward the side of the place. "With that said, I'm checking the whole area."

Bree took out the key she'd found in the

safety-deposit box and unlocked the front door, then thrust it wide. When she entered, she stopped a few feet inside and scanned the main room with a kitchenette and breakfast nook off to the left. "No presents."

David put the supplies down on the counter dividing the living area from the kitchen, then gestured toward the winding stairs to the right at the back. "Upstairs maybe. I'll check while you look down here. Jeremiah could have put them in a cabinet."

David climbed the steps and poked his head through the opening to the second floor, a loft with two doors that led to bedrooms. After checking what few spaces a person could hide something, he went down the winding stairs.

Bree emerged from behind a door on the right side. "That's the bathroom but no presents." She pointed across the cabin. "The pantry has no presents, either, but fully stocked shelves. It doesn't look like we'll starve."

"So what happened to that bag of presents you saw Jeremiah bring to the cabin?"

"The one that would give us all the answers to what's going on? Beats me. But we'll tear this place apart until we discover the answer."

The front door to the cabin opened and his dad came inside, stomping the snow off his boots. "No footprints around except ours." He shut the door. "I notice there's a sturdy lock on this. That's nice. I might sleep well tonight. Any presents?"

Bree shook her head while David said, "No, but it would have been nice if he'd had them under a decorated tree just waiting for us."

His dad removed his heavy gloves and rubbed his hands. "Let's see what we know. Bree watched Jeremiah go toward the cabin with the presents and come back to the plane empty-handed. No footprints in the area. From the weather of this area, it hasn't received any snow since that storm moved through. So that means the presents are still in here hidden somewhere."

"We'll search some more after I let Thomas know we made it." David pulled out his satellite phone and called his friend. "We're here but haven't found anything useful yet. How about you? Any progress on the case?"

There was a long silence. David started to ask if Thomas was still there when the detective said, "We found Sonny Franks this morning."

"Great. Maybe he'll talk."

"I don't think so. He's dead."

TEN

When David said, "Great. Maybe he'll talk," Bree perked up and watched him as he talked with Thomas. The smile that had been on his face almost instantly fell, and he turned his back to her.

Was David talking about Bruce Keller? Or Sonny Franks? Whoever it was obviously didn't give Thomas any information on who was after her.

She walked over to the back window by the fireplace and stared out at the large stack of firewood covered in snow. When was Jeremiah planning to come here? The shelves were stocked and there was enough wood in the bin inside the cabin as well as outside to last a month or two.

What were you up to, Jeremiah?
Where did the money come from?
Why are people after me?

The sound of David saying goodbye to Thomas drifted to Bree. She swung around. Her gaze locked with his, and she didn't like what she saw in his eyes. The news wasn't good.

He covered the distance to her, his shoulders squaring as though preparing himself to impart bad news. "Sonny Franks has been found. He was murdered. His body was in the field behind his house."

"Any idea who killed him?" Bree asked, almost detached from herself—as if viewing the scene from a distance.

"No. There was no evidence at the scene, but they're going through his house inch by inch for any indication of where Gail might be, and they'll keep pressing Keller for information."

"We've got to find what they're looking for. Then maybe we could use it for an exchange for Gail." *If she's still alive.* But Bree couldn't say that out loud.

"That's what we're here for. Let's start down here. How big was the bag of gifts?" Don asked from across the room.

"Like a grocery store paper bag." Bree indicated the size with her hands. "I'll take the kitchen area."

"We'll work on the living room." David held her look for a few extra seconds. "And pray we find something."

Bree started with the pantry but didn't find anything. When she sat on the wooden floor and began opening the lower cabinets, she discovered the cloth bag the presents had been in, folded and stuffed in the bottom series of drawers. She hopped up and waved it. "At least I'm not imagining that Jeremiah stopped here and brought some gifts in this."

With a frown, David rose from looking in the wood bin next to the fireplace. "That means he took the presents out of the bag and hid them somewhere. Why? If this is his place, as we know it is, then why bother to do that?"

"For that matter, why wrap them? Why the big charade? There weren't many people at the runway in Daring to see it. I don't even remember anyone handing the bag to Jeremiah." Her head began to throb, and she massaged her temples. "Why didn't he just tell me about his new cabin and say he was taking supplies or something like that to it?"

"Because he didn't want you to know. The only reason you do now is because he's dead. Otherwise it would probably still be a secret to you." Don got down on his hands and knees and checked beneath the couch.

Bree looked through the cabinet under the sink, withdrawing the large covered trash can. She pulled out the plastic bag and spied some wrapping paper in the bottom. She stood up and dumped the contents on the counter. The red that had covered the top box in the cloth sack tumbled out along with some crushed boxes.

"I found the remains of the gifts, but nothing that was the actual present, unless you like moldy coffee grounds, a few empty cans and a TV dinner." Bree wrinkled her nose at the odor emitting from the trash bag.

Joining her, David stared at the mess. "So he brought the gifts, quickly unwrapped them and then stashed whatever was in one box or boxes somewhere. Did he bring anything back from the cabin that day of the wreck?"

Bree pictured Jeremiah trudging back in the snow, his arms and hands empty. "No. I suppose he could have stuffed something into his coat pockets. I didn't notice a bulge, but then I wasn't looking for one."

"If that was the case, then why come after you? They inspected Jeremiah's body most likely when they came that day after the wreck. If not, they sure did when they took the plane and dumped him under the trees."

Don approached the counter and leaned over to see the trash. "Then it's here in this cabin. We have to keep searching."

As David and Don went back to the living area, Bree swept the trash into the plastic bag, walked to the front door and placed it outside. Making her way back to the kitchen, she scanned the cabin for any idea where Jeremiah would have hidden anything. Nothing stood out, and for a few seconds defeat edged its way into her mind, until thoughts of Gail spurred her on. She had to find it and fast.

After hours searching the cabin, David sought a breath of fresh air, even though the temperature of that air was near zero. Out on the porch, he leaned against the railing and thought back to his so far unsuccessful search for some unknown asset worth killing for. Through the trees David stared at the stream with frozen sections, especially along the sides, and shivered, not so much from the cold as from the lengths these people would go. Kidnapping. Murder.

With the wind picking up, he needed to see to his plane and make sure it was secure a couple hundred yards away by the level ground near the stream. He straightened.

The sound of the cabin door opening and closing drew him around to watch Bree exit, bundled up as though she were going for a long walk. She smiled. "I thought I would join you. I had to get away for a few minutes. The frustration of coming up empty-handed is getting to me. We've checked every nook and cranny.

We know it was here at one time. So where is it, whatever *it* is?"

"A good question I don't have an answer to. I thought after I make sure the plane is okay, I'd walk around and get a feel for the landscape."

"You think he hid it somewhere besides the cabin? He was only gone ten minutes or so."

"There isn't much left for us to check in the cabin. It'll be dark soon, so I won't be gone long." He took a step toward her, then another to close the space.

"Your dad is going to make a fire, but first he's examining the fireplace to make sure nothing was hidden up the flue."

The warmth in her eyes chased away the chill in the air. "We wouldn't want what they're after burning up." He framed her face with his black-gloved hands and said what he'd been thinking for the past few days. "I want this over with so we can spend time really getting to know each other." He knew he should take his words back, but he couldn't, because what he said was true. He was tired of being alone.

"I know this is a stressful time," she replied. "But I've always believed that stress brings out the true nature of a person. Over the past few days, I've learned that you're dedicated to what you need to do. You care about others and your family. Your rapport with your father illustrates that. You're worried about when your daughter shows up, but remember she's coming. She might be ready to mend your relationship. Holding on to anger doesn't really satisfy anyone." Bree clasped her arms around his waist. "It only destroys. Melissa wouldn't be coming to see you just because your dad is here. She could have chosen another time to see him. She didn't."

In all Bree had said, she really didn't address their relationship or them continuing to get to know each other after the ordeal was over. Although she cuddled up to him, he sensed a barrier between them—fear of getting too emotionally involved. After what he'd gone through with Trish, he could understand how she felt, but now he wanted more—with his daughter and most especially with Bree.

"I know I wouldn't be here without you, David," she continued. "You have been beside me from the beginning, but I can't promise anything beyond the moment," she finally said.

He rubbed one of his thumbs across her lips. "I know. Do you trust me?"

"Yes, with my life."

"Everything will work out in the end. I have to believe that." He dipped his head and savored her taste on her lips. Somehow he would make those words come true. They would find what they needed because once they did Bree would no longer be the target.

He pulled slightly away and kissed each corner of her mouth before covering it again. His arms glided down her back to hold her close. "As much as I like this, I need to see to my plane before it gets dark. We wouldn't want to come out tomorrow morning and see it blown over."

"I'll come with you. I need a change of scenery."

He grabbed her hand, and they descended the two steps to the snow-covered ground. He followed their tracks from earlier, and when they reached his Cessna, he removed a drill from the plane to make the holes for the anchors. With Bree's help, he finished with a little light still left.

"Want to explore around the cabin or have you had enough of this cold?" David asked, as he put his equipment into his aircraft.

He turned toward her just as a snowball pelted him in the middle of his chest. She laughed and backed away. With quick reflexes, he bent, packed the snow and threw it at her, catching her arm while she spun around and began running as far as she could in the foot of snow.

"I guess that's your answer. You want to play." He chased after Bree, her laughter music to his ears.

His long strides closed the distance between them, and he leaped forward, tackling Bree to the ground. He rolled with her in his arms until they both were covered with snow. He ended up pinning her beneath him. Their gazes bonded, and suddenly the atmosphere between them changed. He could hear the pulsating beat of his heart in his head.

He released his hand about her wrist and brushed the flakes from her face. Then he leaned down and gave her a kiss that said everything he couldn't really put into words yet. His feelings for her were evolving. He knew if anything happened to her, something would die inside him. With her, his hope had been renewed, and he didn't want to let that go. She made him want to revive his shaky relationship with God, too. Despite all that had happened to her, she still believed in God. That faith came through and challenged him to do likewise.

"If you weren't cold before, you've got to be by now," he said and moved to her side, offering her his hand. "It's getting too dark to explore the area. Maybe tomorrow." After he stood, he tugged her to her feet.

"That is, if I thaw out by tomorrow."

"At least the plane should be okay."

She plowed toward the porch. "I told your

dad I'd help with dinner tonight. You get to clean up."

He scooped up some snow and aimed for her back. Splat. Bull's-eye.

She froze. Then she swept around, scooped up some snow and lunged for the tree nearby while she hurled her snowball toward him, hitting him square in the face. He began stalking her.

She squealed and dashed for the cabin entrance. "You don't play fair."

When she hit the steps, his dad flung open the door, and she raced inside just as David's snowball struck the wall next to her.

"I don't believe I've seen you have a snowball fight since you were a kid." His father moved to the side, and David entered the cabin.

"It felt good to let adult burdens go for a while." David removed his overcoat, looking forward to warming himself in front of the fire in the hearth.

Bree shrugged out of hers and hung it next to his. "Yeah. We should have done that ages ago." She clapped him on the shoulder.

Suddenly he felt a cold wetness as she dropped some snow down his shirt. "You didn't."

"Yes, I did. Thanks to your father, who gave me some. Now we're even." Grinning from ear to ear, she leaned against the door. "And I'm not letting you outside."

He chuckled and sat with his back to the fire to let his shirt dry. "I can't believe my own dad joined forces against me. His son." But David couldn't keep his smile contained. He remembered when he used to play with Melissa in the snow—the times they built a fort or went sledding. Bree was right. He had to find a way to right his relationship with his daughter.

"I won." Bree clapped and pumped her arm in the air. "I didn't realize dominoes was so much fun. Thanks, Don, for bringing your set." She scrutinized Don's face. He averted his gaze, and she asked, "I did win fair and square, didn't I?"

David's father looked right at her. "Yep. I've never let someone win."

The sound of clanging pots emanated from the kitchen as David put them up in a cabinet. Bree glanced into the kitchen. "Does he always make this much commotion?"

"I heard that. I get to play the winner." David dried his hands on a towel, then hung it up.

"That's my cue to go to bed," Don said. "I'll take second watch." He pushed off the couch and headed for the stairs to the second floor. "Tomorrow we've got to find it."

It. That was how they had begun to refer to whatever someone was searching for.

"If it's here, we will." David took the chair across from the coffee table and set up the dominoes.

Bree peered at the blaze that filled the cabin with warmth. "What if it isn't here? What are we going to do?"

"A lot of praying," David replied. "We need to stay here until the police figure out what's going on, and finding it should help them." He drew her attention back to the game once they said good-night to Don. "Let's draw to see who goes first."

Bree's tiles added up to eleven. She grinned. "Only one number beats me."

David flipped over double sixes. "I guess it's my day." He looked up at her and winked. "I got not just one kiss from you and now this." He scrambled the dominoes around the table-top, then began selecting his pieces.

Halfway through a game she was losing badly, Bree checked her watch. "Shouldn't you call Thomas and check in? You don't want to wait too long. Maybe he'll have some good news."

"I'll call when we're finished. Did I tell you I was the one who taught Dad to play a few years ago?"

"Oh, I see. You're a dominoes shark."

Ten minutes later, David laid down his last tile. "Game over."

"I don't think I have to count this up. It wasn't even close. I'm consoling myself with the fact that I played with a master."

David retrieved his satellite phone. "Loser puts up the game and fixes the winner a pot of coffee. I'm going to need it."

He walked toward the door and stepped out onto the porch to make his call. Bree wanted to follow, but she knew hearing only one side of a conversation might lead her to a wrong conclusion. She was going to think positive thoughts. "Thomas has rounded up the people responsible, and Gail is back home with John. Please, Lord," she said as she prepared the coffee.

When David came back into the cabin, she took one look at his solemn expression and knew she didn't want to hear what Thomas had told him. She switched on the coffeepot, then came out of the kitchen, facing David across the room.

"It's bad. What happened? Gail?"

He nodded, cleared his throat and cut the distance between them.

Bree's heart plummeted, and her gut solidified into a twisted lump.

"She's alive," he said, swallowing hard, "but in critical condition."

Tears sprang to her eyes, and through the sheen, she watched him reach out and draw her against him. "The police found Franks's car a few hours ago, and Gail was tied up and gagged in the trunk. She suffered from a gash on her head and hypothermia and dehydration. She's at the hospital now with an officer standing guard at her door." He clasped her upper arms and peered at her. "She's alive. Remember that."

"Any frostbite?"

He inclined his head, his chest swelling with a deep breath. "She may lose her left foot."

Bree's world came to a standstill. She'd done this to her friend. No words came to mind. Nothing but guilt swamped her. Her legs gave way, and David's grip on her tightened.

He held her up and guided her to the couch. "You are *not* at fault here. You didn't do this to Gail. Franks and probably Keller are the hired guns who did. Someone else is calling the shots. Don't blame…yourself."

The hesitation in David's declaration brought Bree's head up. Tears rolled down her face. "You're just trying to make me feel better. I am to blame. Even you must think that. I heard it in your voice."

"What you heard was my realization that

I wasn't to blame for two of my team being killed in that last mission I flew. For over a year I've blamed myself, but I didn't fire the missile at my B-52 bomber. That was a terrorist on the ground. I haven't been able to shake the thought that the lieutenant who was killed had two young children who will never know their father."

"Were you able to fly back to base or did you crash?" She remembered the emotions that had run through her when she'd gone down, not knowing if she would survive or not, especially when she saw the trees rushing toward her.

"I managed to land, but we were attacked by a ground group. We took what cover we could find until help arrived. My lieutenant was next to me when he was shot. I'll never forget the look on his face. It haunts me at times. I tried to get back to the base, but it wasn't possible."

The grief in his words mingled with her own, and it was her turn to comfort him. Loss was never easy to take, but when someone felt responsible, it was worse. Her arms entwined about him, and she held him close as though she could absorb some of his pain from the memories. She'd been there before and knew what those thoughts could do to a person—replaying it over and over in his mind, trying to figure out how he could change the outcome.

She took in his face, which had become so dear to her. Combing her fingers through his hair, she said, "We can't usually control others' actions. In fact, there isn't a lot we can control but our response and attitude. I know that in here—" she pointed to her head "—but in my heart I can't seem to grasp it."

"Because knowing and feeling are two different things. You feel responsible for Gail's injury because you think it should have been you. You know that you can't control what really happened to Gail, but feelings are hard to dismiss."

"What if she loses her foot to frostbite?"

He pressed a finger over her mouth. "No more what-ifs. There are many possibilities good or bad, but there will only be one outcome and at the moment the doctors don't know it. Remember your visit with John. He doesn't blame you, so why are you? I can't imagine you blame yourself for every patient's illness you treat."

"I wouldn't last a month if I did. I've learned that in order to survive as a doctor."

"There are times in our work we have to separate ourselves from the tragedy in order to do our jobs. I had a long talk with Thomas once. He sees a lot as a police detective. I did as a soldier, and now as a SAR volunteer. You do as a doctor."

"I hear what you're saying but…" How did she explain because it was personal it was different?

"You can't be everything to everyone. You can't fix every problem." One corner of his mouth quirked. "Now if I would just listen to what I'm telling you."

"Again we're back to knowing versus feeling. Sometimes there's a wide gap between the two."

He put more space between them and clasped her hands. "But we can pray for Gail. God is the one who can help her."

Bree bowed her head and said, "Please, Lord, heal Gail and save her foot. She is in Your hands now and those are the best ones for her. Also please help bring the people behind this to justice. In Jesus Christ's name."

"Amen." David looked at her. "We're doing all we can, Bree. Get a good night's rest and we'll start again tomorrow." He bent forward and gave her a light kiss.

Bree headed up the stairs and took the room where she had stored her bag. She walked to the window and stared out at the forest nearby, the white snow on the ground lightening the surroundings. The cabin was located in a beautiful spot. She could see why Jeremiah bought it.

Jeremiah, what have you done?

* * *

The next morning, armed with his gun, David headed to his plane to make sure the ties had held and everything was all right; then he would explore the forest surrounding the cabin. Some of it was hidden by the thick spruce trees, and he always liked to know the lay of the land, especially if they were going to stay for a while.

The one thing he hadn't told Bree last night was that Thomas told him that Keller made bail and had disappeared. No sense having her worry about Keller when David would do it for the both of them.

Satisfied his Cessna was fine, David trudged toward the line of trees as the sky began to lighten with dawn approaching. He'd needed a break after they'd finished another unsuccessful search of the cabin. As Bree and his dad were about to begin again, David had decided it was time to make sure his plane had weathered the high winds through the night and then look around. And then he still had to look around for any place nearby that Jeremiah might have used to hide what was in the bag.

The silence of the forest calmed him as he walked through the trees. *The quiet is in stark contrast to the sounds of a combat situation.* That thought popped into his mind, and he realized why. His confession to Bree last night.

He'd never told anyone how he'd felt after that skirmish where he'd lost two of his men. She had that effect on him. He was used to holding feelings inside, but surprisingly he'd felt better after their talk. Maybe that was his problem, keeping everything inside.

Suddenly the silence he relished was disturbed by the sound of rotor blades like on a chopper. He glanced up through the branches of the trees and spied a white helicopter zooming toward the cabin. He raced toward it, watching as the chopper touched down in front. Breaking free of the forest at the rear, David still had a hundred yards to make it to the back of the cabin. The sound of gunfire chilled him to his core. Then an awful quiet followed, one that declared the possibility of fatalities—Bree and his dad or the intruders.

He didn't even bother trying the back door. His dad kept it locked as well as the front. But the shots had come from inside. His legs pumping as fast as he could run in the foot-high snow, he rounded the front, glimpsed the busted-in door and the helicopter lifting off. The sight of Bree slumped against the window of the chopper, pulling away, fueled David's fury. Before he could decide what to do, a man in the chopper peppered the ground with rounds from an automatic weapon, forcing him back behind the side of the cabin.

In seconds the intruders were gone. David didn't know if he could face what awaited him inside. With dread, he mounted the steps and stepped through the doorway. The first thing he saw was his father stretched out on the floor, blood pooling on the wooden slats.

ELEVEN

At the feel of leather against her cheek, Bree stirred. The motion of the chopper vibrated beneath her. She kept her eyes closed, hoping to glean something before they knew she had awakened from the tranquillizer they'd shot her with. At least she was alive, but for how long?

A hand nudged her. Over the noise of the helicopter, a man said into her ear, "I know you're awake. I suggest you take it slow and easy as you sit up."

She stayed where she was.

Fingers gripped her. Her eyes flew open. A thin, tall man with a scar down his left cheek pulled her up and shoved her against the back door.

Again he stuck his face in hers. "You've cost me a lot of time and money. I'm tempted to open that door and push you out."

Fear jammed a fist down her throat.

"I've lost a couple of good men because of you."

Coffee-flavored breath assailed her nostrils. Her stomach roiled. She might never appreciate coffee after this. "How did you find me?"

"There was a tracker in the side of your medical bag. We know how important it is to you and hoped you would take it with you." A sinister smile spread across his face. "And you did." His grip dug into her. "I won't hesitate to kill you if I don't get what my boss wants. He isn't a nice man."

Her throat tight, she murmured, "What?"

"Diamonds, worth millions. Jeremiah stole them."

Her head still groggy from the tranquillizer, Bree closed her eyes, trying to compose herself. But only one thought replayed in her mind: *I've seen his face. He'll kill me once he gets what he wants.*

David rushed to his dad's side a few feet inside the cabin. Don moved and groaned, raising his hand to his head where a deep gash bled freely.

"Take it easy." David scanned his father's body and found another wound, a bullet hole in the fleshy part of his leg. It wasn't bleeding as much as the head injury, which meant an artery hadn't been hit.

Neither wound was fatal. Relief trembled through David as he assessed the cabin. Another man, who fit the description of Keller, lay to the left of his father, a bullet hole in his chest. David reached over and checked the man for a pulse. There was none.

"Stay still. I'm calling Thomas, then carrying you to the plane."

His dad tried to lift his head and nearly passed out again.

"That's why you don't move."

"Bree?" His father licked his lips. "Where is she?"

"They took her." David bolted to his feet and went into the kitchen where he'd left the satellite phone. When Thomas answered, he told him what happened and that he would be at his hangar in ninety minutes. "I need an ambulance. Dad has been shot and has a head wound."

"We'll see if we can pick up the helicopter's flight path."

"Anything. Even a general area. I'll find Bree." Because he had to. He should have been here. Guilt inched into his mind. He shoved it away. He wouldn't let guilt immobilize him.

He crossed to the bathroom and found Bree's medical bag where she'd put it yesterday. He hurried back to his dad and tended to the two in-juries, hoping the bleeding stopped. After ban-daging the leg, David checked the head wound and gave thanks when he didn't see any blood coming through the white gauze.

"C'mon, Dad. I'm taking you to the plane. You can lie down in the back. Okay?"

"Yes. I'm tough."

David looked around for anything he might need, then gingerly scooped up his father into his arms and left.

"Got to shut the door," his dad murmured.

David didn't see how he could with his nearly two-hundred-pound father weighing him down. "I don't care about the cabin."

"You must come back…find the diamonds… That's what they're after… Bree's life for them." His father raised his dangling arm and pointed toward the opening.

David stepped back. His dad fumbled for the knob and managed to close the door. Then he passed out.

David walked as quickly as he could to the plane and ten minutes later was in the air head-ing toward Anchorage. He'd never moved as fast as he did unhooking the Cessna and leav-ing the tie-downs and anchors there. It looked like he would have to return to use the dia-monds as a bargaining chip. He placed a call to

Ella at Northern Frontier and asked her to call Chance. He needed help once he made sure his dad would be all right.

Teeth chattering because the three men in the helicopter hadn't bothered to grab her coat, Bree focused on the landscape below the chopper. If she could escape, she wanted to know the best way to go to find help. But so far she'd seen few signs of civilization. At least she figured they were heading southeast. Anchorage? If they were, she might be all right. Help would be nearby at least in the city.

Then the helicopter veered directly east, flying over the Alaska Range with Denali in it. Maybe Fairbanks was their destination. That would be okay, too. But then the pilot took the chopper down low, skimming the tops of the trees, no doubt off radar. In a clearing with one cabin, he set the helicopter down. For miles she saw nothing but this cabin, as isolated as Jeremiah's was.

Her spirits plunged. It was up to her to escape and then pray she could make it through the wilderness to help. When her door opened, a man grabbed her arm and dragged her from the chopper. She stumbled and went down to the snow-packed ground. He hauled her to her feet and shoved her toward the cabin. She assessed her chances of running for the woods, then instantly dismissed that idea. With the snow, it wouldn't be hard to track her, and with each member of the trio armed, she wouldn't make it two feet. They would probably shoot her in the leg so she couldn't escape. That was if they didn't kill her.

Putting one foot in front of the other, she trudged toward the cabin, following the tall, thin captor while the other two were behind her. The hairs on her nape tingled as though their gazes were drilling holes into her.

I can't do it without You, God. Please send help.

As she crossed the threshold into the cabin, the guy who had seemed to take pleasure in manhandling her earlier in the chopper propelled her forward with a rough push until she fell onto a ratty-looking couch, her cheek pressed against a scratchy cushion. The odor—a mixture of cigarettes and mold—emanating from the sofa turned her stomach. She thrust herself up to a sitting position and peered up at all three men surrounding her. A wall of menace caged her and pinned her against her seat as if she were a butterfly captured and put on display.

Thin Man glared at her. "You have caused us a lot of problems."

Good.

"You were with Jeremiah that last day. What did you do with the diamonds? They aren't at his place or yours. Where are they? Your life depends on the right answer."

Saying she didn't know wasn't going to work. Frantically, she thought of the right answer. If she knew where the diamonds were, she would gladly give these men all the gems.

The burly man who liked to shove her encroached into her personal space. Her eyes grew wide as they locked on his raised fist. She swung her attention to Thin Man. "I don't know anything about diamonds. Today from you is the first time I heard about them. Obviously I don't have them. You've searched my house."

"And the clinic."

Bree gasped. They'd searched the clinic. When?

"That means you put them somewhere else."

An idea teased her mind. It might work. She slouched her shoulders as if resigned. "Okay. They're in a safety-deposit box Jeremiah had."

Thin Man's eyebrows rose. "So now you know where they are. You're lying. We have connections. You discovered some bonds but nothing else. The police are checking into where they came from."

How does he know that? Granted the contents weren't a secret, but still... "Is that why you took the plane? To look for the diamonds?"

His glare sharpened on her right before Thin Man nodded to the burly one. The next thing she felt was a fist hitting her jaw. Her world swirled before her eyes.

David stood with Thomas in the ER hallway while the doctor examined his dad. David's gut knotted with the tension that had spread throughout his body since arriving at the hospital. Before that, he'd had to hold it together and focus on getting his father the medical care he needed.

"I haven't had a chance to tell you the clinic where Bree works was ransacked last night," Thomas told him. "The cleaning crew came in around eleven and found it trashed. They immediately called us. No drugs were taken, which means they were looking for something else. In particular the office Bree shares with several doctors was thoroughly searched, more than the rest of the place. The clinic closes at seven so it happened between that time and eleven." Thomas folded his arms and lounged against the wall next to David.

He glanced sideways at his friend. "I won't be surprised if my home is next."

"Last night I sent a patrol car to sit outside

your house. This morning I removed the patrol officer from the area but had a lookout posted in your neighbor's place. Nothing so far."

"According to Dad, these people are searching for diamonds so we must be dealing with a smuggling ring. How much, he didn't know, but obviously a lot if they're going to this much trouble. They want the diamonds in exchange for Bree."

"There's quite a black market for blood diamonds from Africa especially. They even forge papers so the gems can be sold in the United States. Lucrative business. The diamonds are smuggled out of Africa for little money but bring in millions once 'legitimized' with a certificate and sold."

"Kidnapping and murder follow these diamonds." David shook his head. "I hope they try getting inside my house. It'll give us someone to pressure for answers since Franks and Keller are both dead."

The doctor emerged from Don's room and approached David. "He'll have a complete recovery. He's lost some blood, has a concussion and a bullet wound that didn't do too much damage. He took a nasty hit to the head, so we'll keep him overnight. That's what I'm worried about the most."

"Can I talk to him?" David pushed off the

wall, trying to keep his anger contained. He needed to remain calm and in control in order to find Bree.

"Yes, he's awake. We'll be moving him to a permanent room soon."

After the doctor left, David went in to see his dad with Thomas right behind him.

After he'd ascertained for himself that his dad was okay, he turned his attention to Bree. "Dad, Bree is missing, and I need information to find her. The helicopter was on radar until it went off the screen around Denali. It finally came back on for a short time, then went below radar again. I have people searching the area in planes, but it covers a lot of acreage. Without the helicopter sitting by where she is, I'm not sure we can find the place. You told me a few things in the plane, but I'd like you to share it again."

His father frowned, then grimaced as though even that action caused him pain. "They haven't contacted you yet?"

"No."

"I think the reason I'm alive is because they wanted me to pass on a message. You have thirty-six hours to find the diamonds or Bree dies. They'll be contacting you about a place to exchange Bree for the diamonds tomorrow at five o'clock."

"Which gives us thirty hours to find the diamonds or Bree."

His dad closed his eyes for a few seconds. "They know the police will be involved—" he looked up at David "—but warned about keeping them back from the exchange. Son, they won't keep her alive a minute past five. The man in charge had no emotion on his face, even when one of his guys was shot. He left him behind."

"If Jeremiah was flying the diamonds from Daring to Anchorage, then his plane or cabin are about the only places the diamonds could be. They didn't find them in the plane, so that means they're in the cabin. I'll fly back there with Chance, and if I have to tear it apart board by board, I will."

"Good. Get going. Time is ticking." His father ran his tongue over his lips. "And send in a nurse."

David left with Thomas, flagged down a nurse, then walked from the ER. Outside the wind cut through him, and he prayed Bree was warm. He turned to his friend. "I'm hoping we find them and I'm back first thing tomorrow. I need to go now, so I don't land at the cabin in the dark. I'll take my phone with me and keep you informed. Since it's no longer a secret where we're staying, I'll write down the coordinates for you. Call with any news, bad or good."

Thomas handed him a pad and pen, then stuck them back in his pocket after David scribbled the location on the paper. "We have several leads we're looking into. One involves a sighting of the white helicopter near the area. A man called the state police about someone buzzing his house. He said the chopper flew so low it rattled some things in his place and one of his wife's favorite plates fell and shattered."

"Keep me posted. See you."

As David drove toward the airport, he thought for a moment someone was following him, but the black SUV turned several blocks before he reached the private airfield. He didn't think the bad guys knew that Jeremiah had made a stop at the cabin, so he might be able to find them and therefore have some control over getting Bree back alive.

He pulled into the hangar and saw Chance talking with Ella. Their somber expressions highlighted the gravity of the situation and sent his heart beating rapidly.

Bree's head dropped forward, and she snapped up, straightening herself in the seat she was tied to. Her jaw throbbed from where the brute had hit her twice until she passed out. When she'd awakened hours ago—or at least she thought it had been that long—she didn't have to feel her cheek to know it was swollen.

The least of my worries.

Exhausted from lack of sleep and fear, she scanned the darkness about her. A blackout shade was pulled down over the sole window, and the only light in the bedroom was a narrow slit coming from under the locked door. It threw the area around her into shadows, but she could make out a bed and a table next to it.

The worst part of all this was they had left her alone as if they didn't need her to find the diamonds. Which made her dispensable. The thought sent panic through her, her heart racing so fast, her breathing came out in pants.

Calm down. If I'm dispensable, they would have killed me at the cabin or after their little chat earlier.

Suddenly the words in the twenty-third Psalm came to mind. "'Yea, though I walk through the valley of the shadow of death, I will fear no evil; for thou art with me.'" She repeated it over and over.

Finally, thirst and the need to visit the restroom overcame her fear, and she shouted out, "Hey, I'm in here." She yelled it again at the top of her voice.

The door slammed open, and the big man she called Brute filled the entrance.

"You must have a death wish," he grumbled and moved toward her.

David stood at the cabin window looking out the back. The state police would be coming later today to take Keller's body back, but Chance had processed the scene yesterday before they'd started looking for the diamonds. He and Chance had torn the cabin apart, especially the floor, looking for any cubbyhole filled with diamonds. Nothing. In another hour, dawn would break. They had run out of places to look for what could possibly save Bree's life.

"Want some coffee?" Chance asked him from the destroyed kitchen.

"Yes." David's gaze swept over the snow-covered ground outside. "When it gets light, we need to check around the cabin. That's the only place we haven't searched. Jeremiah had about ten minutes to hide the diamonds. The stash has to be close even if it's outdoors."

The satellite phone rang. David had set it on the mantel. He snatched it and said, "Please have good news, Thomas."

"Have you found the diamonds?"

"No."

"We think we found where they're keeping Bree. I'm organizing a raid. I'd like the diamonds as a backup if there isn't any way we can extract her without endangering her life."

"We're checking outside next. I can't think of another place inside. Maybe we have this all wrong."

"Let's hope not."

"How's Dad doing?"

"I checked on him this morning like I promised. He's chomping at the bit to get out of the hospital. The doctor wants to keep him for a while longer."

"And Gail? Any news there?" David took the mug of coffee Chance handed him and drank several swallows.

"Better. The doctors are hopeful they can save her foot."

"Good. We'll keep searching here and see you soon."

David ended the call and faced Chance. "Thomas thinks they found the place they're keeping Bree. We have a few hours to find the diamonds and get back to Anchorage. We're going to use our flashlights. It won't be as good as in full daylight, but we're running out of time."

"Sounds good to me. I can't stand around and not do something anyway."

For the next hour as the sun rose, David examined every crevice that could possibly hold a small bag of diamonds. Discouraged, with time running out, he rose from checking where the rear deck connected with the cabin. He stretched and rolled his shoulders as he decided what was left to search.

His gaze fell upon the reserved log stack at the line of trees twenty yards from the deck. Snow had laid a white blanket over it. Undisturbed, but then the snowstorm had passed through this area, too, since Jeremiah had been here.

David hurried toward it. It actually wasn't that bad a place to hide some diamonds. Even if they got wet, they would be fine. He began tossing one log after another to his side. Near the bottom, he saw what he had been looking for. As he reached through the hole he'd created in the stack, excitement surged through him. His fingers grasped the big brown pouch and pulled it free. When he peeked inside, his heartbeat pounded against his chest.

The diamonds glittered in the sunlight slanting through the trees. Big gems. Small ones. He'd never seen so many in one place. He stuffed the pouch in his pocket and hastened to find Chance and leave. His friend was searching in the front of the cabin.

David rounded the corner and held up the pouch. "Let's go. We don't have much time."

Chance descended the stairs of the porch. "Where?"

"The log stack at the back of his property."

David did his check before taking off while Chance hopped into the front passenger seat. *Lord, please let us be in time to save Bree.*

Grumbling under his breath the whole time, Brute untied Bree, gave her some water, then escorted her to the restroom across the hall and stood guard outside the door. While inside, she refused to look at her bruised face in the mirror because she would have little time in here. Instead, she examined the window, set high up the wall, to see if there was a way to get out. She stood on the toilet and unlocked the window, then stepped down to flush and turn on the water at the sink. When she returned to try to push the window up, it wouldn't budge.

This was when she wished she had some strength in her arms. *Note to self: if I ever get out of this situation, I'll take up weight lifting.*

The sound of pounding on the door reverberated through the small room. "You have half a minute to come out."

She tried again one last time. Finally it inched up. She pulled it down, scrambled off the toilet and stuck her hands under the water, then opened the door. She shook her arms. "There are no towels in here. If possible, next time can I have one?"

"This is no hotel," he said with a few curse words thrown in to demonstrate his irritation. "If you don't watch it, there might not be a next time. Sit," he said when they were back in the bedroom.

She did and smiled up at him. "Thanks for doing that." *Establish a rapport with your captor.* She thought she'd read that somewhere. Besides, anger wouldn't help her and would drain what strength she had.

He snorted and went behind her to tie her wet hands. When he pulled tight, she gritted her teeth and kept her hands apart as much as possible.

"What time is it?" she asked as he headed for the exit.

"Your friends have eight hours to find the diamonds or…" He slammed the door shut.

Her heart skipped a beat, and she began repeating Psalm 23.

David settled in behind Chance and Thomas, hidden in the forest surrounding the cabin where Bree was believed to be. David had given Thomas the pouch of diamonds when he'd arrived at the hangar, then had played the message on David's cell phone he'd received while out of range. It had been made from a throwaway phone. The kidnapper would call again at five to tell David where he was to go to make the exchange. The message had been followed up by a photo of Bree. Right now, the memory of the photo gripped him as though a grizzly had him in his paws. His chest constricted.

"Everyone is in place," Thomas said in a low voice.

"What's your plan?" Impatience made David antsy.

Chance glanced at David. "I'm going to try to get closer and see if I can see inside to determine if Bree or the kidnappers are there."

"Let me go with you. I might have been a pilot, but I've had experience with these kinds of situations while serving."

Thomas clasped his shoulder. "No. You have to stay back."

David ground his teeth and clenched his hands. He watched as Chance covered the open space between their hiding place and the cabin on the right side.

Flattening against the outside wall, Chance rose up on his toes, trying to see into the high window. "Can't see anything," he whispered over his com link. "Checking the front window." He rounded the cabin and, crouched over, ran to it. After peeking inside, he retraced his steps to the right side. "There's a tall, thin man like the one David described and a large muscular guy. This is the place."

"Move around the cabin and check the window on the back side," the commander overseeing the raid said into the com link.

David, who could listen but not talk, leaned toward Thomas. "There were three men beside the helicopter pilot. Where is that third guy?"

Thomas spoke to Chance about locating the third assailant.

Noticing the shadows, David glanced at his watch. Two-thirty. "Sunset will be soon, and if they really are going to trade Bree for the diamonds, shouldn't we make our move?"

"The best time would be when it gets dark. We'll move in then unless the helicopter comes before sunset. We'll have to assess whether to move in or try at the diamond drop in Anchorage, but since we won't know the drop site ahead of time, it'll be hard to set up around the perimeter there."

David was glad he'd brought his night vision goggles. "Any message from your police officer answering my phone about the exchange?"

"No. I doubt they'll call until five."

"If you raid the cabin, I'm glad to see one

right side with a window high up, probably the bathroom, and the left side with no window. That means they can only keep an eye on the front and back. Not your best place to protect."

"But they were counting on us not finding it."

A tight grip of stress held him. David tried to relax his muscles, especially in his shoulders. He kneaded them, then his aching neck. He was thankful that Thomas had made sure Gail and his dad were protected as all this went down. Maybe by this time tomorrow everything would be over with.

As darkness settled over the terrain, David used his night vision goggles to scan the area. Chance had no way of confirming where the third man was. That bothered him.

TWELVE

Bree worked to loosen her hands, the skin around her wrist raw and bleeding from the rough twine. She focused on the pain and used it as a motivator to free herself before Brute came back to check on her. He usually popped in every thirty minutes, at least he had for the past couple of hours. Finally the ropes fell away, and she attacked the ones around her chest that pinned her to the hardback chair. Thankful her feet were left free, she bolted from her seat and went to the window with the blackout shade. She'd rather climb out of it than the one in the bathroom.

It was not only locked but nailed down. It would take her too much time to work the nails out of the wood. She whirled around and hurried to the door into the short hallway. Holding her breath, she put her hand on the knob and prayed the door was unlocked and Brute wasn't posted outside the room. Slowly she turned the handle and then eased the door open a crack to peek into the corridor. Clear.

The sounds of voices from the living area urged her to act now. With a fortifying breath, she hurried to the bathroom, slipped inside and locked the door. She clambered on top of the toilet and inched the window up. Once the space was wide enough for her to crawl through, she gripped the ledge and hoisted herself up onto the sill, using the toilet paper dispenser as a step. As she pushed off, it crashed to the floor. For a few seconds she froze, clutching the wooden sill.

Using the front tips of her shoes, she walked a few inches so she could turn and drop to the ground below the window. The door crashed open, and her glance over her shoulder collided with Brute's gaze, full of rage.

"What do you mean I can't go with you on the raid?" David whispered to Thomas in a furious voice.

"You're a civilian. I can't allow it, but I'll do everything I can to protect Bree. Stay out here in the trees. Promise you won't try going into the cabin unless I signal or call for you."

David glared at his friend, clamping his lips tight.

"If not, I'll have to leave someone back to

keep you safe. Do you want me to go in with one less man?"

"I promise."

"Thanks," Thomas said as he slipped into the darkness surrounding them.

David put on his night vision goggles and followed the seven-man team as they made their way toward the cabin. With only one door, they would all use the front entrance. He wouldn't go on the raid, but he would circle around to the back where there was a window low to the ground. Somebody needed to monitor it, in case one of the kidnappers tried to escape that way.

David kept to the trees as he weaved through the forest to the rear of the cabin and set up observing the right side with the high window and the back with the lower one. No one was going to get away if he had anything to do with it.

Settling behind a large trunk of a bare tree, he scanned the area. The sound of the battering ram striking against wood echoed through the small clearing, followed by gunfire and shouting. It took all his willpower to remain still.

Movement at the high window on the right side of the cabin caught his attention. It looked like a body emerging from the window. He zeroed in on the person. *Bree*? He rose and took a step forward. The sound of a gun being cocked, then the feel of a barrel against his back riveted him to the spot.

A loud crash, then the rat-a-tats of a barrage of bullets spurred Bree into action. Adrenaline zipping to every part of her, she propelled herself through the opening, but Brute's grip clamped around her left ankle. Without thinking, she rammed her booted foot into his face and plunged down toward the earth nestled in a snowy blanket. The howl of his fury resonated through her head as she smashed into the ground, her left shoulder taking the brunt of her fall. Pain shot through her like a bullet.

She couldn't let that slow her down. She jumped to her feet and surged toward the woods on that side of the cabin. With a look back, she spied Brute diving out of the window and hitting the snow, then rolling. Up in an instant, he raced toward her. She pumped her arms and legs as fast as she could. The darkness of the forest yards away dangled safety before her. If she could hide…

She heard his heavy breathing behind her right before he flew into her and slammed her into the ground. The air swooshed from her. She struggled to get a decent breath. She wasn't going down without a fight. With the thought of seeing David again, she twisted and kicked until Brute sat on her and pinned her arms down in the snow. Using every reserve of energy she had, she bucked and writhed, trying to dislodge the man, but the pressure of his bulk on her chest kept her from taking full breaths. In seconds, darkness began to swim before her eyes.

There was the sound of a gun going off nearby, and Brute jerked toward the noise coming from the left. As Brute moved, he came up and off Bree. Air flooded her lungs. Making use of the momentum of him rotating to the side, she toppled him, shoving him off her. She rolled away, then clawed her way to her feet while he righted himself. She dived into the line of trees, determined to find a hiding place in the night's blackness. It was her only chance.

Not daring to slow down to look back, she moved as quickly as she could with her arms out in front of her to stop her from running into a trunk. She heard Brute behind her, then a loud thump as though he'd collided with something. Praying he had, she kept going. She only began to slow when she realized she couldn't hear him behind her anymore.

She chanced a glance over her shoulder. Only black and the far-off lights from the cabin greeted her. As she turned forward, she ran right into a thick branch, stopping her in her tracks. She sank to her knees, teetered, then crashed into the snow.

As David dropped to the ground, he twisted around and went for the person's leg behind him. The sound of the gun going off thundered through his head, and he felt something graze his cheek. Rage filled him. He plowed into the shooter and took him to the ground. They rolled in the snow, and his opponent ended up on top of David. The man, bigger than him, still grasped his revolver. He brought it up to aim at David.

He gripped his attacker's wrist and squeezed with all his strength, but the gun remained in the man's hand. Slowly as they wrestled for control of the weapon, it inched closer toward David. Through his night vision goggles, he saw the fierce determination to kill him written on his assailant's face. The sight fortified his own resolve.

Suddenly the man rose a few inches and came down on David's chest. All air rushed from his lungs. He heard and felt a rib crack, and pain stabbed him in his chest. For a couple of seconds, his grip loosened on the weapon.

In that momentary lapse, the gunman pointed the weapon at David's chest. As his attacker pulled the trigger, a surge of adrenaline zipped through David's body, and he managed to move the revolver slightly. The bullet hit his arm. More pain flooded him.

From somewhere deep inside, David found a burst of strength to knock the weapon from the man who momentarily—for only a second—slackened his grip on the gun. The assailant's eyes widened as the revolver flew through the air. His gaze followed the trajectory, which gave David the opportunity to pull his Glock from his pocket.

When the man looked back, David had the gun aimed at him. "I'll kill you if I have to."

The attacker smiled at the instant he went for David's weapon. He shot the assailant. His body was suspended for a few seconds before he toppled over onto David, sending waves of pain careening through his arm. Despite that, David shoved the guy off him.

His wounded arm throbbed as his adrenaline rush began to fade. He felt the man's neck. Relieved he was alive, David pushed to his feet, found the other weapon, then went in search of Bree. His only goal was to find her and make sure she was okay.

He righted his askew goggles, then made his way to where he'd last seen her fleeing the cabin. Inside his coat sleeve the wet warmth of his blood ran down his arm. Light-headed, he followed the trail of footprints in the snow into the forest.

Quiet reigned until he heard a moan. He hurried his pace and discovered a huge man on the ground by a large tree. David lifted his gun as the man's eyes opened, then shut. He had nothing to tie the guy up with. David glanced behind him and saw Thomas enter the forest.

"I'm over here, Thomas."

His friend hastened to him. "You're shot. This guy?"

"No, another one." David motioned deeper into the forest with his good arm. "I think Bree got away and this man was chasing her. I'm going after her now that you're here."

"I don't think you're in any condition to go after her."

"That's not an option." David trudged forward, trailing the footprints in the snow. "Bree," he called out several times, listening to his voice echo through the trees.

As he progressed, blood dripped off his hand onto the white snow. His vision blurred, and he wanted to rip off the goggles, but he couldn't. Trees, often close together, were like a maze that he had to weave through. How did Bree do this in the dark?

"Bree," he shouted again, then listened.

As he dragged gulps of freezing air into his

lungs, his chest protested. His head seemed as if it was swirling like a kaleidoscope. When he stumbled, he caught himself before going down by clutching a bare branch.

Then he saw Bree on the ground, lying still. His heart lurched, and he hurried his steps. When he reached her, he dropped down beside her and checked to make sure she was alive. Her pulse beat beneath his fingertips.

"Thank you, God," he murmured.

He swayed and crumbled to the side, a black void swallowing him.

Her head pounding, Bree stirred on the cold ground. Pinned beneath an arm, she panicked and pushed away. She felt a sticky substance covering her hand. *Blood*?

She felt the body next to her. Not big enough for Brute. When her fingers traced the face, she encountered goggles and removed them from the man's head. Using them, she saw David in a weird green light, red smeared on his cheek, the left sleeve of his tan coat now crimson.

She scanned her surroundings and a movement in the distance caught her attention. *Thomas*? If David was here, then other rescuers were, too. She took a chance because David needed help.

"Over here," she yelled. Then she opened his

coat to check how much damage had been done to his left arm.

"Bree, you okay?" Thomas asked, coming upon her and kneeling on the other side of David.

"Yes, but he isn't. He was shot, and he's losing a lot of blood. Also, something grazed his cheek. Let's get him back to the cabin where it's warm and call for a helicopter. He may need surgery."

Thomas spoke into a com link and a few minutes later help arrived. Still woozy herself from running into a big limb, she let them carry David toward the cabin while she walked next to them, trying to clear her head so she could tend to his medical needs until the helicopter came.

The sight of David lying there limp in the arms of the men, his eyes closed, threatened her composure. *Please, Lord, he's got to be okay.* But in the back of her mind the whole way, she thought she was responsible for him being hurt. He'd saved her life and had been dragged into a situation he hadn't bargained for.

Hours later, she observed the surgery on David to remove the bullet. Her forehead had a goose-egg-size bump, and the doctor on duty insisted she stay in the hospital overnight. She agreed she'd stay only as long as she was watching David's surgery. She wasn't promising anything beyond that. She took a couple of pills to dull the pain hammering against her skull in a thundering cadence.

When the surgeon finished with David, he glanced up and said, "He'll be fine. But I'm not sure about you. You look pale. Go. Sit. I'll find you in the waiting room."

"But—"

"Bree, it isn't a request. I insist. I'll be out to talk to you and his family. Cheryl, see that she follows my directions."

One of the nurses disengaged from the group around David in the operating room. Bree didn't wait for her to approach. She left, barely putting one foot in front of the other. Everything seemed to be crashing down on her finally.

In the hallway, Cheryl walked with Bree. "I hear Gail is doing better. I praised God that they were able to save her foot. She should be leaving the hospital by tomorrow."

"Thanks for letting me know. I'll go see her after David is settled and awake." Bree stopped outside the waiting room. "I appreciate all the staff has done for Gail, David and Don."

As Cheryl left, Bree leaned against the wall and bowed her head. *Thank you, Lord, for their recovery. I can't believe so many people were hurt because of me. I'm at a loss what to do. How can I face them when I know what happened to them*?

She chewed on her lower lip as she glanced to the side at the entrance into the waiting room and saw Don. She sighed. He'd tried to protect her at the cabin when those men had kidnapped her and he'd been shot. Because of her. Trembling, she hugged her arms to her. All she wanted to do was hide and shut down emotionally.

"Bree, I thought I saw you in the hallway." Don filled the doorway into the waiting room. "You okay?" Using his crutches, he came to her. "You need to sit. The past few days have taken their toll on you."

And not you? But when she peered into his craggy face all she saw was concern and sympathy. "You don't need to worry about me. You're the one who was just released from the hospital and has a son admitted."

"Come on in and sit with me. I've been so worried about you."

"About me?" The whole time she'd been held captive she'd wondered about Gail, Don and David. She hadn't known if Don or David had survived the shoot-out at the cabin.

"Yes, of course. You were kidnapped. I've worked my share of abductions, and I've seen the trauma the victims go through. I doubt you've even had time to process anything. You're probably feeling shell-shocked."

She nodded then started for the waiting room before she collapsed in the corridor. All the strength in her body seemed to be draining away. After sinking into a chair across from Don, Bree slouched back.

"Thomas was just here to let me know the progress of the case." Don took his seat and laid his crutches to the side. "A few of the men are talking, and he's confident he'll round up the smuggling ring in the next few days."

"Oh, good," Bree murmured automatically.

"Now that the police have the diamonds, he's sure you'll be okay. You can start putting your life back together, but Bree, that will take time. I've never been kidnapped, but any trauma that knocks the feet out from under you affects you deeply. You can't run from it. I tried when I lost my wife suddenly. The pain and memories caught up with me. And I suspect my son is still dealing with the trauma of his last tour of duty. I know, because I served in Vietnam." He reached out and covered her hand with his. "David was a different man after Trish's death, and then he went back to the combat zone and that changed him even more. A person, even a strong one, can take just so much before something gives. But remember the Lord is there for you the whole way. You aren't alone."

Don smiled, a soft mellow one. "You should rest. You look like you've been up for the past forty-eight hours."

"I'm a doctor. We're used to it in an emergency." She wanted to dismiss the exhaustion slowly weaving its way through her body. "I can't leave until I make sure David is all right after the surgery."

"I understand the operation is pretty routine. He's a tough guy. He'll be fine."

"But I know what can go wrong even in a routine one." She began remembering a few cases where a problem developed at the end of surgery or in recovery. Her heartbeat increased, and perspiration beaded her forehead and upper lip. She jumped to her feet, intending to go back and see if David was in recovery yet.

Don called her name as she strode toward the doorway. She glanced back to tell him where she was going when she collided with David's surgeon, Dr. Neil Baker.

He steadied her, then made his way to Don. He waited until she returned before he said, "Your son will be fine. He shouldn't have to stay in the hospital but a day or so. You can go back and see him in fifteen or twenty minutes. The nurse will come get you." Neil's gaze lit on

Bree. "We have a bed for you. You won't be officially admitted, but I would like you to hang around. That is one big bump on your head."

"I know what to look for, and if any signs of my concussion worsen, I promise I'll be back."

"Then after you see David, both of you go home and sleep. Half the night is already gone."

"We will," Don said, looking pointedly at Bree. "Won't we?"

She ginned at his mock intimidation. After Neil left, she added, "You need to work on that tough look."

With his arm in a sling, David stood at the window in the living room, staring at the snow as though Bree would materialize in it. She had been there in the hospital, taking care of him, even taking over for the nurses. He had to admit he'd enjoyed the attention, but behind her professional facade he sensed something was wrong. According to Thomas, the case was netting them numerous arrests with the discovery of the smuggling ring that specialized in illegal diamonds brought into the United States via Russia. He'd hoped she would relax some with that news, but when she heard, she began to withdraw.

Now she was coming to see him, and he felt like a teenage boy waiting for his sweetheart to show up. That thought took him by surprise. When had he started falling in love with Bree? Probably that morning when she'd crawled out of the snow cave and looked up at him. But he realized when he was trying to rescue her from the kidnappers and he knew he would put his life on the line for her, that he was determined to pursue a relationship.

When her car pulled into his driveway, David headed for the front door. The sight of her as she walked toward him accelerated his pulse rate. He leaned toward her and gave her a kiss, then ushered her inside.

"It's so good to see you, especially outside the hospital," he said in the foyer, drawing her closer to give her a kiss that expressed his new-found feelings.

She turned away and walked into the living room. "Where's your dad?"

"In his room resting, or so he told me after he heard you were coming."

"He's not upset with me, is he?"

"No way. On the contrary, he thought we needed some alone time."

She blushed and averted her gaze while she took a chair.

That left David the choice of the couch or the other lounger, neither next to her, which was where he wanted to be. Definitely something was going on, and he couldn't blame Bree with all she'd been through. He eased down on the coffee table, not far from her.

"How have you been?" she asked, busying herself with placing her purse on the floor next to her.

"Recovering." He shrugged. "What's a little pain when we're responsible for bringing down a smuggling ring?"

She finally lifted her gaze to his. "You were shot. Your dad was, too."

"And you were kidnapped. That's the past. I've looked back on my past too much. Not anymore. I'm moving forward. Dad told me this morning about your concern with us getting hurt helping you. Please don't. The alternative was letting you get killed. That is unacceptable. I would never have forgiven myself. I'm not carrying around that kind of guilt again. I finally got over my feelings of responsibility with Trish's death, and I'm putting the last mission in perspective. The only thing you control is your actions, your attitude. Not mine or my dad's. Or even Gail's."

She flinched. "You're certainly blunt."

"Only the truth between us. I've held my feelings inside for so long. I don't want to with you, and I don't want you to feel like you have to with me. I love you, Bree. I don't need months to decide that."

Her shiny eyes widened. "I…I don't know what…" She bolted to her feet and started for the foyer. "I need to see Gail, then meet the lawyer at the bank."

He moved the fastest he had in the past couple of days and clasped her arm before she opened the front door. "I'm not pushing you into anything, but I did want you to know how I feel. I realize this ordeal has taken a toll on you. I'll give you all the time you need."

She twisted around to face him, his grasp on her slipping away. "Don't. I care about you and that's the problem. Whoever I care for—love—dies. You nearly did, along with your father." She grabbed the handle and thrust the door open. "Goodbye."

"Bree, Melissa will be here in a couple of days. I hope you'll meet her and join us for Christmas dinner. Dad's cooking."

Her back to him, she shook her head and descended the steps, her strides long as she hurried toward her car.

When she disappeared from view, he came back into the house and shut the door.

"Since she didn't stay long, I gather it didn't go well with you two."

David looked up to see his dad in the hallway. His observation was an understatement. "I think I blew it. I told her I love her. It didn't mean anything to her."

"Oh, I think it meant something to her, and that's the problem."

John let Bree into his house with a big smile. "Gail's been expecting you. Now that you're here, I'm gonna run to the store. I shouldn't be gone more than twenty minutes. She's in the den."

Bree made her way to the den while John left. Her friend sat in a lounger with a blanket over her legs. "It's great seeing you at home."

"I know. That's how I feel. Come, sit in John's chair. How are you doing?"

"Me? I came to ask you that. You're the one who has been in the hospital."

"Because my injuries were physical, but that doesn't mean you don't have wounds that need healing."

"I'm fine. I ran into a branch that left this on my noggin," she gestured to the knot on her forehead, "but other than that I wasn't hurt."

"So it was no big deal you were kidnapped? It was to me."

"That's not what I meant. Yes, of course, it was a big deal."

"It's okay to admit you're hurting emotionally. That you're scared. That you never felt that much fear before. That the only thing that kept you going was you knew God was with you every step of the way."

"That's how you felt?"

Gail nodded. "Still do. It makes me feel vulnerable, but also I realize the Lord is there for me—and you."

"But look at what happened to you, David and Don, and it all started with me being in a plane wreck. It snowballed so fast my head is still spinning."

"Yes, exactly, but John told me how you felt. You. Did. Not. Do. This. If you have to blame someone, blame the men after you or even Jeremiah."

Jeremiah. "As his activities in the ring unfold, I'm stunned I didn't know the man really."

"You knew one side of him. He worked hard not to reveal the greedy side to you. Thomas told me he built up a nice nest egg for himself. You know what? I believe that last day he realized he wasn't right. He didn't want you involved with the diamonds he was transporting so he hid them at the cabin. He planned to fly you to Anchorage, then come back for them later."

"I don't know. I want to think he was trying to protect me. But what he did for years was wrong."

"Yes, and he needs to be forgiven."

"Can you?" Bree asked, her feelings still too bruised to know how she felt about Jeremiah.

"I'm working on it."

"That's all I can do, too." *Is Jeremiah the real reason I pulled back from David when I love—* Her thoughts pulled up short. *I love him?* The realization sent a tidal wave of joy through her that she couldn't—didn't want—to stop.

"Bree, what's wrong?"

Bree smiled. "I just realized I'm in love with David. How's that possible? I haven't been with him for long and certainly that time wasn't reality. I was so wrong about Jeremiah, who I knew for years. What if I make that kind of mistake with David?"

"You think he's smuggling diamonds?"

"No. I mean…" Bree tilted her head and stared off into space for a moment. "I don't know what I mean. I've seen David under difficult circumstances, and it's hard to disguise your true self when you're running for your life."

"Yeah, it does kinda strip life down to the bare bones." Gail shifted in her chair. "To answer your questions, all we can do is our best when making decisions, but life is a risk. We'll make good decisions and bad ones. There is no way around that, but search your heart and go with that. Love sometimes comes fast, sometimes slow. Snatch it when it does, either way."

John stood in the entrance into the den with a brown sack in his hand. "I've got the ice cream you wanted," he said, then disappeared down the hall.

"Ice cream?" Bree teased her friend. "It's twenty degrees outside."

"My indulgence, no matter what the weather is like. Want to join me?"

Bree chuckled. "Normally, I'd jump at the chance but—" she glanced at her watch "—I have to meet Mr. Anderson at the bank in half an hour. I'll come back another day for some."

"You've got yourself a deal. It probably won't be this carton since I doubt it will last more than a day or so in this house."

Bree came over to Gail and hugged her. "I'm praying for your fast recovery."

"I'm praying for you, too. Remember, David has been there for you, and I never got the impression he didn't want to help you."

"Thanks."

As Bree drove toward the bank where she was meeting Mr. Anderson, she thought of the last time she'd gone there with David. That was when she had realized the possibility that Jeremiah might not be who she thought he was. Maybe in the paperwork the lawyer needed there would be an answer. For all she knew Jeremiah had stolen the Eurobonds. Was he planning to leave the United States?

She wished David were with her for this. Going to the safety-deposit box even for a short time wasn't something she wanted to deal with right now. Too much, too soon.

She pulled into the parking lot, switched off her car and sat gripping the steering wheel. She thought of calling David, but with his arm disabled, how would he even get here? She could do this. It would probably only take about ten minutes to photocopy the bonds for Mr. Anderson and the police to help them investigate their origins. Then she would give the lawyer the deed to the cabin, Jeremiah's insurance papers and anything else he needed to work on the estate. *Ten minutes. I can do this.*

When she entered the bank and walked to the area to check in, Mr. Anderson rose from a nearby couch. Carrying a briefcase, he approached her with concern on his face.

"You've had quite an ordeal over the past couple of weeks. I won't keep you long. I know this can't be a pleasant task, but I want to move forward on the estate and get everything wrapped up."

"Frankly, at the moment I want nothing to do with Jeremiah's estate, but I'm sure I can come up with a way to use any money from it for good use." The one thing that consoled her was the clinic she worked at could use the money to treat more people who couldn't afford medical care. Maybe out of all of this some good would come.

"I don't blame you. I talked with the detective handling everything. He filled me in on the past few days. He wanted to make sure there wasn't anything else he was missing concerning this case. I hope not. I want to give the detective a clear picture of Jeremiah's estate. Like you, I've discovered the man wasn't who we thought."

"You said you two were friends. How long did you know him?" Bree signed the card and gave the woman her key to the box.

"I've known him for years on a casual and business level. I always handled anything legal for him."

After the bank employee unlocked the large box and slid it out, Bree took it and followed the woman to the small private room for the patrons. "Let's get this over with."

When the woman left, Mr. Anderson backed up to the door while Bree opened the box. She picked up the ten Eurobonds and turned to the lawyer. He held a gun on her.

* * *

David sat on his couch and reread the same page three times. He slammed the book closed and set it on the coffee table. This inactivity was driving him crazy. He was stuck in the house, not able to drive or fly his plane. Ella was keeping him informed about Northern Frontier SAR. But the worst part of all of this was he wanted to be with Bree, helping her through her pain and disillusionment with Jeremiah. But she didn't want to have anything to do with him. The tight pressure in his chest expanded.

David's cell phone rang, and he rushed to answer it. He needed to be distracted from his thoughts. "How's it going, Thomas? Got everyone?"

"Almost. That's why I called you. I tried Bree's cell phone first, but it went to voice mail. She isn't with you, is she?"

I wish. "No, she left a while ago and went to see Gail. What's up?"

"I've had one man who dealt with the head guy of the smuggling ring finally accept a deal. Mr. Anderson, Jeremiah's lawyer, is who he claims ran everything. He has for years. I wanted to warn Bree since she had dealings with the man. I'm leaving the station and on the way to his office to arrest him."

As David listened to Thomas, dread hardened in his gut. He was on his feet and striding toward the kitchen, where his dad was, as he said, "After seeing Gail, Bree was meeting with Mr. Anderson at the bank."

"Then that's where I'm going." Thomas hung up.

The sense of urgency pushed David. He was much closer to the bank than Thomas was. "Dad, do you think you can drive? Bree is in trouble."

"Sure." His father grabbed his crutches and started toward the hallway to get his coat. "I only need my right leg. But what are you going to do with a bum arm?"

"I don't know. But she needs to be warned and protected from Mr. Anderson. He runs the smuggling ring."

"The one time we have to be injured," his dad muttered as he slipped on his coat and headed for the exit.

David retrieved his revolver and followed after his father from the house.

After all that's happened, I pray I'm not too late, God. Protect her.

Bree's heart thumped against her rib cage, her gaze glued to the gun pointed at her. "Why?"

"Because it's only a matter of time before one of my men the police have been rounding up let them know I'm the head of the smuggling ring, especially since they caught one of my top guys. I'm practical and a survivalist, and that means I have to leave the country now." He gestured with the weapon at the safety-deposit box behind Bree. "Eurobonds worth a million is a good start for me. You don't even want the money, so don't make this difficult. You'll go with me to the airport, where I have a plane ready to take me to a country where the United States can't touch me. If you cooperate, I'll leave you in the trunk of my car, where I'm sure the police will find you eventually."

Like Gail who nearly froze to death. The thought shuddered down her length. "What do you want me to do?"

"Hand me the Eurobonds. Carefully. The rest I don't care about."

She did as he said, and he slipped them in an inside coat pocket.

"The one thing I love about these is they are easy to transport. Let's go. Stay right next to me and remember I have a gun pointed at you. I don't think you want someone innocent to be hurt because you did something foolish."

As they walked side by side with Bree slightly in front of Mr. Anderson, she felt the barrel of the weapon pressed into her ribs. When they stepped outside and made their way to the parking lot, every muscle tensed in Bree. She calculated her chances of getting away from the lawyer now that they were outside and fewer people were around. But she couldn't come up with anything that didn't end with him shooting her in the back.

Nearing a white sedan, Mr. Anderson slowed his step. "That's my car. I want you in the front seat driving until we get away from the bank. If you try anything, I have nothing to lose if I kill you."

Fear swamped her, and she stumbled on a clump of ice.

The lawyer's grasp tightened. "Keep moving."

"I'm trying," she said through clenched teeth.

When Bree was a few feet from the driver's side, she reached to open the door.

"Drop the gun or I'll shoot you." David's voice came from behind them.

A calmness she hadn't experienced in days washed over her.

Mr. Anderson shoved the gun barrel into her back. "Not if you don't want me to kill her." He swung around with Bree plastered against him with one arm across her chest to hold her in place. "I'm leaving with her."

David lifted his arm and pointed his revolver at the lawyer's head. "In the military I won many awards for my marksmanship. Normally a shooter goes for the biggest body mass on a person, the chest, but not me." His lethal tone conveyed his determination. "You won't survive."

"Neither will she," Mr. Anderson retorted as the parking lot filled up with patrol cars and officers getting out and aiming their weapons at him.

"You won't get away." David's tense, fierce bearing showed him to be a man used to combat.

Bree heard the lawyer's breathing increase. She felt his chest rising and falling rapidly. This wouldn't end well unless she could think of something to end this stalemate. She stared at David, so focused on Mr. Anderson, and wanted to tell him she loved him, no matter what.

Then an idea came to her, and without another thought Bree totally went slack, her body sinking to the pavement as though she'd fainted. When her body touched the parking lot, she rolled into the lawyer, throwing him off balance.

David charged the man, while he tried to recover command of the situation, and knocked the gun from Mr. Anderson's grasp. The officers were all over the lawyer, putting him in handcuffs and dragging him away. David helped her to her feet and with one arm drew her against him.

"I love you, Bree. I'll wait as long as you want, but I need you in my life."

She leaned back, words escaping her at the moment. All she could do was stare at his dear face and thank the Lord for bringing David into her life. "So much has happened and I feel like my head is swimming with it all."

"I understand—"

She pressed her fingers over his mouth. "But I do know I love you. We can work the rest out later when we've both healed."

He bent down and kissed her, a perfect one that told her everything she needed to know. David was her soul mate.

EPILOGUE

"You're up before Grandpa," David's daughter said as she came into the kitchen on Christmas day.

"I told Dad I would put the ham on." David slipped the roaster into the oven and shut the door.

"You?" Melissa said with a laugh.

"Yes, only because Bree and Dad prepared it last night before we went to midnight service."

"Oh, that explains the offer."

"Want some coffee?"

"Did you make it?"

"I'm not that bad, but your grandpa put it on last night. All I had to do was plug it in."

"Sure. We haven't had much time to talk since I arrived, and I want us to before Bree comes and Grandpa gets up."

David tensed as he poured two mugs of coffee. He never knew what to expect from Melissa since she'd become a teenager. Now was not any different, although since she'd come to Anchorage, their relationship had been pleasant—no drama, no arguments. He thought maybe that was because Bree had been part of a lot of their activities. Melissa and Bree had gotten along from the beginning, which had thrilled him.

He took a chair across from his daughter at the table and slid a mug to her. "What do you want to talk about?"

"Us. For so long I blamed you for Mom's death, but I have a friend at school who is dealing with a similar situation with her boyfriend, and I saw how he tried to fool her that everything was all right. He nearly died from an overdose of painkillers from a football injury. He's getting help now. She didn't realize for a long time what he was doing." Melissa drew in a deep breath. "Mom made the decision to do what she did, not you, and I wasn't fair to you about it. I lashed out at you."

"I did my share of stuff wrong. I should have been there for you two more. For a long time I thought my career was the most important thing in my life. Your mother even encouraged me those last few years to rise in the ranks in the air force."

Melissa's eyes filled with tears. "That last time you went overseas, I was so angry but also hurt that you did."

"I want us to start over and build a relationship from here on out. Can we?"

One tear slipped down her cheek, and she brushed it away. "That's why I came. I'm realizing how important family is, and we have a small one."

David rose and came around to hug his daughter. With Melissa and Bree in his life, this would be the best Christmas ever.

"I didn't think the holidays could get any better, but it just has," his dad said from the entrance. He joined them, enclosing his arms around David and Melissa. When his father stepped back, he drew in an exaggerated breath. "What great smells to wake up to—coffee and ham."

When the doorbell rang, David hurried to answer it. The second Bree entered, he took Ringo from her and put him down on the floor; then he pulled her into his arms. "This is the first Christmas for us as a couple, with many more to come."

Bree chuckled. "No, you don't get to open your present until later when everyone else does."

"But I should have been able to open it on Christmas Eve." Joy enveloped David, something that had been elusive for years—until Bree came into his life. "Please now." Ringo rubbed against his leg, demanding attention, but David only had eyes for Bree.

She shook her head. "Okay, but only after I open my gift first."

"Wait right here." David went into the living room and found the small box under the tree. He brought it back to Bree. "I hope you like it."

She tore into the package and revealed a glittering solitary emerald on a gold band. "Yes. Yes."

David had started to get down on his one knee and stopped. "Who told you?"

"I did," his dad said. "You know I can't keep secrets like that." Next to his dad in the hallway was Melissa with a big smile on her face.

David turned back to Bree and knelt in front of her. He had to ask her formally. "Will you marry me when you're ready? We can wait six months, a year—"

"How about a wedding on Valentine's Day?"

He rose and pulled Bree to him. "We can wait longer. I want you to be sure."

She threw her arms around him. "I am sure. My present to you is getting married this Valentine's Day." Then she gave him a kiss that sealed the rest of their lives.

* * * * *

Dear Readers,

The Yuletide Rescue is the first in my Alaskan Search and Rescue Series. I have several books planned for this series, and the next will be out in February 2015 titled *To Save Her Child*. I've always been fascinated with Alaska and loved the time I visited my friend who lived there. The state has such contrasts and covers a huge area. Alaska will be a great setting for a series centered on search and rescue missions.

I love hearing from readers. You can contact me at margaretdaley@gmail.com or at P.O. Box 2074, Tulsa, OK 74101. You can also learn more about my books at www.margaretdaley.com. I have a newsletter that you can sign up for on my website.

Best wishes,
Margaret

Questions for Discussion

1. Trust is important in a relationship. Both David and Bree have trouble putting their total trust in God. Have you put your total trust in Him? If not, why not?

2. Bree is self-reliant and depends on herself. Do you consider yourself independent, needing no one? Is it possible to go through life like that?

3. Bree tries hard to control her life, to have it planned, so there are no surprises. She finds out that isn't always going to work. Life often throws a person a curve ball. How well do you deal with changes in your life? Does change scare you? Why or why not?

4. What is your favorite scene? Why?

5. Bree is devastated when she finds out about Jeremiah's illegal activities. Have you ever had someone fool you for months or years? What did you do when you found out what was really going on?

6. David can't forgive himself for his wife's

suicide. He felt he should have seen the signs and been able to do something to help his wife. Have you ever felt responsible for someone else's action? How did you deal with it?

7. Jeremiah betrayed Bree, and his actions put her life in danger. If someone did that to you, could you forgive the person? Why or why not?

8. Who did you think was behind the smuggling ring? Why?

LARGER-PRINT BOOKS!

GET 2 FREE
LARGER-PRINT NOVELS
PLUS 2 FREE
MYSTERY GIFTS

Love Inspired®

Larger-print novels are now available...